I0672740

LOST
GRAVES

LOST GRAVES

A NOVEL BY
Franklin Lafayette King

*t*P

Texture Press
2014

Lost Graves
Copyright © 2014 Franklin Lafayette King

All rights reserved

Published in the United States by
Texture Press
1108 Westbrooke Terrace
Norman, OK 73072

For ordering information,
visit the Texture Press website at
www.texturepress.org.

ISBN-13: 978-0-615-95463-9
ISBN-10: 0-615-95463-4

Cover painting and photographs by Franklin L. King
Poems, unless otherwise noted, are by the author

Book design by Arlene Ang

This is a work of fiction. Names, characters, businesses, places, events
and incidents are either the products of the author's imagination or
used in a fictitious manner. Any resemblance to persons, living or
dead, or actual events is purely coincidental.

All rights reserved. No part of this publication may be reproduced,
stored in a retrieval system, or transmitted in any form, or by any
means, electronic, mechanical, photocopying, recording, or otherwise
without either the prior written permission of the publisher or the
copyright holders. This book may not be lent, hired out, resold or
otherwise disposed of by way of trade in any form of binding or cover
other than that in which it is published without the prior consent of
the publisher.

FRIENDLESS CHILD

To dwell in chambers ornate,
where room, book and chair do speak.
Hallways of shadows do appear to greet
the young traveler's wandering voyage.
Do not look too deep nor linger too long where shadows live.

Loneliness does proceed and follow steps
so soft upon wooden floors swept of laughter and smile.
Mirth does not dwell in rooms so bare where only objects converse.

Muted voices from ages past
sound from walls of photographs and acrylic art.
Mirrors reflect curtain-drawn rooms dressed in dust-streaked light.

Hearth not lit nor merry voice of stranger sounds.
Untouched house in perfect array awaiting
the moment of decline and decay.

House of rooms where spiders dwell in regal splendor
from molding cracked by the prairie's relentless swell.

Friendless child accompanied by wooden soldier and antique plane.
Small hand upon that which does not respond
to voice so soft in halls of shadows and soundless rooms.

His only friends: metal toys placed upon wooden floors in unlit rooms.

Dedicated
to

CHRISTINE

TABLE OF CONTENTS

PROLOGUE

While I am a believer in good and evil, my religious convictions prevent me from interpreting the events that transpired in the house that was moved from Dahlonega Street to Mt. Ebal. It is important for these facts to remain isolated from my own beliefs. What happened or why it did is left to the reader's interpretation. I have found from my own experience that a person should not look too deeply into dark rooms or stare at antique mirrors. My hand writes this story as one whose fingers are placed upon a Ouija board. I know not what direction or answers it will provide.

I am a collector of antique books. One day when attending a trade day in the foothills of the Appalachian Mountains, I felt the stare of a vendor. I have always been sensitive to people looking at me. Perhaps it comes from having excellent peripheral vision or a sixth sense. The vendor motioned me to come to his stall. There I noticed an unimpressive collection of old books. Many of them had been bestsellers depending upon the decade in which they had been published, their gaudy outer jackets fragmented by time. None of the books, however, interested me. The vendor, therefore, asked me what type of book I was looking for. I mentioned either a very old volume dealing with early Alabama architecture or one with an unusual or striking cover. Regardless, it must be a leather-bound book.

He asked me why the binding was important and not so much the content. I replied that I had just installed some nice bookcases in my house, and with a smile, that I wanted to appear more intellectual than I actually was. A fact I didn't mention to him was that I like the odor and feel of old leather books. I've always found pleasure in spending time in the rare book rooms of academic institutions.

The vendor walked to the back of the store and, upon his return, handed me a leather-bound volume to examine. Without opening it, he replied that he had bought it from a young woman that happened to be attending trade day just this past week.

It appeared to me to be a diary of some kind. I could barely read *My Visit to Mt. Ebal House, 1863* written in ink on the outer binding.

I then opened the small leather book. The first few pages were simply notes related to the planning of a party. The handwriting was accomplished in beautiful calligraphy. As I flipped the remaining pages, I noticed the mentioning of a journey to New Orleans aboard the *General Foster*.

I am so excited about my trip aboard the steamer. After three days, we arrived in the Port of New Orleans. My brother took me to Jackson Square to see the shops with all their fine imported European clothes. You can't believe the gown that I bought. It will be perfect for the Mardi Gras ball at Colonel Eliot's later in the season.

While walking about Jackson Square, Phillip said that it would be fun for me to have my fortune told. You know how adventurous I am. As we entered the shop, it smelt just like lavender. While Phillip looked at some books, an aged woman who appeared to be a Creole led me to a back parlor. In the recesses of the shadowy room was a young woman who was apparently very sick since she did not stir upon my approach even though I extended my hand in formal greeting. She remained motionless yet I could feel her stare. Forgive my imagination, but I had the strange feeling that she was not real, like a carving rather than a person.

The teller of fortunes asked me what I wanted to know. Of course, I told her about John, and that we were planning to be married in Mobile. Since John and I have talked about a family, I asked her how many children we would have. She told me in a most crude fashion, "You have a child." When I said that I did not, she said that the child was I. Can you imagine such insolence? As she spoke, I felt strange like the air within the parlor had changed, almost suffocating. For a moment, I thought that I was the young woman who was lying upon the couch. I told Father about it when we arrived home. I don't think I will mention it to John since it is a matter of honor.

I have not been feeling well since New Orleans, I must make a note to ask Dr. Abner C. King about it. I don't think I have been sleeping soundly, such terrible dreams.

The rest of the journal listed what had been purchased while in New Orleans until I came to the last page. There were only three lines: Colonel Jeffery Phillip Renfro, CSA, 1838 – 1863, Miss Annie Fuller Finch, 1840 – 1863 and Lieutenant Gregory Fuller Haynes, CSA, 1840 – 1863. At first, this meant nothing to me. As a result of the age and binding, however, I purchased the book and placed it high on my newly installed bookcase. There it was to sit until after the Palm Sunday tornado.

Later, I visited the Alabama Rare Book Room located on the top floor of the university's library. The room itself, kept locked, was seldom made available to patrons except upon the request of a scholar investigating the early history of the State. Being newly employed in the history department, I was anxious to visit the collection.

After being admitted to the collection for the first time, I immediately noticed flags, photographs, paintings and early maps that hung upon the walls of the large academic chamber. I then scanned the volumes that lined the shelves preferring a physical observation of the titles rather than the computer-generated catalog. There were many volumes referencing the War Between the States and the early industrialization of Alabama. At the end of one of the stacks, I noticed a book that looked very familiar to me. Upon dislodging it from its firm position, I examined the volume carefully. The title of the book was *My Visit to Mt. Ebal House, 1863.*

At first, I was very disappointed. I immediately thought the book that I had purchased at trade day must have been one that was mass-produced under the same title. It too was probably intended to be a ledger or a diary. This book, however, was very different from the one that I had earlier bought. The strong smell of decaying leather was very apparent. As I opened it, I noticed that it contained several small jackets intended to hold daguerreotypes. Even though photography had been perfected prior to the War Between the States, mass-produced photographs had not been. It was very odd to me, therefore, to find such an old book that allowed for their display.

I immediately put the book upon a desk, cut on the green banker's lamp, and began to study the daguerreotypes inserted into the jackets. There were four images of a Greek Revival cottage, from various angles, that sat upon a slightly out-of-focus rise. Huge trees were behind the house while another view showed a side angle of the cottage that included both sky and distant mountains. In the three photographs, there were varying views of formal gardens outlined by well-trimmed box hedges. Wisteria plants had wrapped around the veranda columns. There on the side porch were three indistinct figures. Somewhat blurred; probably because of their inability to remain motionless as required in the creation of this early type of photograph.

On the next page, there was only one daguerreotype. The other jackets were empty. The photograph was of two men and a woman in a formal pose. Two of the people were in focus while the third and larger male figure was slightly blurred as a result of his having moved during the exposure process.

The woman in the photograph was seated in a classic wicker settee. Both men stood behind her. What interested me most was that the partially blurred individual looked amazingly like Professor Jay Renfro who was a full professor in my own history department. I flipped through the remaining pages only to find them empty of any content. The names, dates and diary entries that had appeared in my previously purchased book were missing.

Obviously the content had not been published and, therefore, the previous owner of my diary had written in the names, dates and other information. I planned on mentioning my find to the professor when I returned to the department. I thought that Professor Renfro would enjoy seeing the photograph made even more interesting by the fact that one of the people in it carried his last name and looked very much like him. The Library's policies forbade my checking the book out. Unfortunately, I did not remember the volume again until much later; an oversight that I will regret for the remainder of my life.

- 1 -
PURCHASE

As Professor Renfro drove down Dahlonega Street, he noticed a FOR SALE sign in front of a very old home. What attracted him was the odd balance of the house and the heavy ornamental portico. It might be classified by some as a Greek Revival cottage. The house sat uneasily upon its sloping lot. A lot filled with ancient cedars that added to the lonely feel of the house. Having always loved the past, the Professor continued to drive by the house daily only to notice that it remained for sale.

The house possessed a past that even a person that was not a history buff would have found fascinating. It was considered to be one of the earliest, if not the first, home built in the small frontier community. In all probability, it was constructed prior to 1835 when Indian nations surrounded the settlement – a time of unrest intensified by the frontier spirit and the conflicts of competing cultures.

The house on Dahlonega Street was absent in the pre-1900 wide-angled photographic shots of the community. This fact bothered the Professor who meticulously searched for images of its earliest existence. Politicians, judges and professors were to later make the house on Dahlonega Street their home following the War's destructive conclusion. A friend of the Professor had even been born in the house.

Upon entering the cottage, there was a feeling of profound sadness. The structure conveyed a strong sense of abandonment and impending destruction. The faint scent of lavender would greet him upon his entry into the hallway. The front parlor floor had separated from the wall allowing the Professor to look outside when kneeling. Wasp and other insects hummed incessantly about the large faintly lit rooms. The beautiful antique windowpanes provided distorted images of the outside world. The Professor could not sense whose world he had entered or what time period the present had become.

The only item indicating the identity of the previous occupant was a photo album. As the Professor scanned the album, there were photographs of two young women and an older woman. The color dyes had shifted as was typical of Polaroids made in the 1960s. It was apparent that the album had been abandoned just as the house had been. He wondered what could have happened to cause the two young women to leave the album in such a conspicuous place. It had obviously been left behind deliberately.

When the Professor visited the house, he always felt that someone else was there as well. A strange sensation like sensing the presence of shadows that dwell in dark corners. He would frequently turn around as though he expected a person to appear. Instead only silence accompanied him as he walked from room to room.

The bathroom had been painted entirely black, while the marble upon the kitchen countertop had been hit so hard by an unidentified object that its surface consisted only of fragments. He knew that even to the most innocent of observers, it was apparent that tragic events had occurred within these rooms.

◌ℬ

As his work as a professor of history continued, his drives past the structure became less and less frequent. Thoughts of the house were lost in committee work and the pursuits of pleasure in the small southern town that he, after his move from Texas, was beginning to be a part of.

In that the Professor had failed to express an interest in purchasing the house, it soon found its protectorate in the form of several area clubs and heritage associations. While their intent was honorable, funds to save the house were not forthcoming. It was finally purchased by two local residents, relocated and opened as a gift shop. The house, however, had been placed within the borders of a proposed shopping mall to be composed of a drug store, grocery store, pizzeria and other privately owned businesses. The house set uneasily waiting for further delivery from destruction.

Once again, the agony of decision rested upon the Professor. Not to save the house would stain his conscience with guilt for he had learned early in life to love inanimate objects. Much like the tenets of Shintoism, he sensed that life was in all things. This he reasoned was a reflection of the loneliness in his childhood when wooden and metal toys were his only companions.

If he did not react, who would save this beautiful yet melancholy and very much out-of-place structure? The days moved by with indecision. As he drove past the house, now loaded onto a moving platform, it sat forlornly on the side of the road, one part on the pavement and the other in a drainage ditch. Surely, someone would torch it or at least break the beautiful antique glass windows.

Whenever he stopped to inspect it after work, he would see the reflection of his face within the windowpanes, an image distorted by the antique glass. The house waited patiently for him.

Earlier, the Professor and his family had searched for a place in the country to build a home. After many months of driving through the surrounding hills and mountains, he discovered an ideal place just far enough from the university to ensure their privacy. As a result of his Ulysses-like search, he purchased fifteen acres in the country.

He had hoped to someday build upon the site that had such a lovely command of valleys and distant mountains. A house had previously been built on the spot so leveling the lot would not be a problem. He did realize that there was no public water source available at the location. The Professor would be dependent on a well whose water had an iron-colored tinge to it. Anyone that used the water for any prolonged time would notice a change in the color of their hair. In addition, the land had been marked with large meaningless depressions. When he asked the realtor why such depressions existed, he only replied that they were test pits for iron ore.

Had he not owned the land, he probably would not have committed to the restoration project. After having previously purchased the land, the Professor acquired a Burlington Northern caboose that had been the victim of a train wreck. Both ends of the caboose showed severe metal compression. Other than the couples and end platforms, the remainder of the caboose was in excellent condition. He always enjoyed reading what was posted on both exterior doors: *Watch Out for Slack Action.*

One morning while he was writing, he was disturbed by various voices from a line of people passing very close to the open windows of the caboose. In that the Professor owned the land, he could not figure out why so many men, women and children were walking past. He did not want to confront any of the visitors that morning about the issue since he intended to have a good relationship with his new neighbors. When later he had the courage to ask a nearby resident, the neighbor replied, "They go to the top of Mt. Ebal to pray each Sunday."

Finally, the Professor committed to the project. For a very small sum of money, ownership of the house was transferred to him. He had sixty days to remove the home from the edge of the planned shopping center or it would, through implication, be bulldozed into the earth.

Without fanfare, the structure began its ten-mile journey into the rural countryside. Landowners had to be consulted since several trees needed to be cut down to make way for it. When one owner hesitated to give his permission, the house spent several nights in a sorghum field until he relented and the tree blocking its path was cut down. Throughout the journey, two end chimneys remained attached to the house.

It was a true engineering accomplishment to have moved the two outside chimneys to the base of the mountain that would be its final resting place. Inch by inch, foot by foot, the house was pulled and pushed up the steep hillside to the flank of the mountain. Upon arriving at the building site, the two end chimneys with their slave-made bricks crumbled and fell to the sides of the house.

There, like a falcon's nest, the house rested awaiting a proper foundation, a foundation it had not had for more than 150 years. An elderly black man soon laid the stones in a proper fashion and the renovation commenced. Free men did the work previously done by slaves.

Extra care was taken not to disturb the spirit of the house. No modifications were made except in the installation of new plumbing and wiring to code. The Professor painted the inside of the structure, running his hand along each portion of the wall, feeling the texture of its surface. The wood felt smooth and cool even in the summer's heat. As a person would love another, so he loved the house.

Can a man be possessed by an empty building? He knew the answer but did not express it. The house communicated its needs, and he responded without concern for those about him.

Each day, he picked and arranged in bowls of china, the wild flowers that crowned the ancient mountain's summit. The evenings were spent in painting the interior of the house in colors that had been favored by the planting class and in watching the moonrise etched by the fluted columns. Occasionally, when the moon was full, he would observe its beams reflected on magnolia leaves.

As time passed, the Professor knew he needed to live nearer to the university. Besides, his whole life was centered about the academic community. As he sat in his study, he wondered if he should mention to any potential renter the secret of the house; a tell told by the Cherokees and later settlers. The secret was not very romantic he knew, but it was relevant to anyone wishing to live in it. The house was located on the path of historical tornadoes and killer storms that killed indiscriminately. He knew that with all of the technological advances, that when the power failed, the pathway to a warning had ceased.

He had grown up in the tornado alley of Texas. His mother and grandmother did not have any warning systems except their keen eyes and the changing scent of the air as black clouds raced towards them as they fled to the earthen storm shelter.

"Best to let sleeping dogs lie," he thought. There was no need to mention an event that probably would not happen again. Yet as he looked out his window, he could see the deep depressions left in the hillside where great trees had been uprooted in the last century. He knew the town at the foot of the mountain had vanished in a funnel in the late 1800s. "No, better not to cause any concern. I need to rent the house, move back to town, and that is that," he muttered to himself.

When the first prospective renter and his wife were scheduled to visit with Professor Renfro, a violent thunderstorm occurred. The potential renters called and said they were hesitant to get out in the storm. The lightning lit the walls of his home followed by the violent clap of thunder. Water ran down the eaves and filled the depressions beneath the windows. It was perhaps their collective concerns that prevented their visit. "No more will be heard from them," the Professor thought. "The house will soon sit vacant, or I must stay to protect it."

The Professor sat again the following day in his home office at Mt. Ebal. Large trees and clinging English ivy darkened the room. Lost notes and silent songbooks from a past century lay in unplanned fashion about the room. Silently, sunlight entered the chamber turning the old leather bindings to amber. The light rapidly touched the desk as his reading glasses created geometric prisms of light. He turned his palm upwards and felt the presence of the sun. Holding the golden rays that would not stay; touching and releasing all too quickly as the source of all life moved into the shadow of the mountain.

The Professor knew inwardly that he would have to continue to look for a tenant. He was no longer comfortable in the house at Mt. Ebal. Over the last two years, he had felt a growing unease in living there. To his dismay, he now realized that he would, in all probability, need to stay longer until a proper occupant could be found. He loved the house too much to sell it. Yet he knew that vandalism and theft would occur to any house left unattended; especially to one in such a remote area.

He realized that his prolonged stay at Mt. Ebal, however, would make an ideal time for him to continue on his research projects. Perhaps even finish an article that he needed to submit for merit pay, a perfect setting, quite pastoral and free from the tensions of the university's competitive environment. Yet the uneasiness remained. As a result, he positioned his desk so that it faced the open room. Behind his desk was a wall full of mirrors placed there by the former owner. There was something about mirrors that frightened him.

Life had become a habit for the Professor. In his desire to be efficient, he felt that each workday's routine should be perfected and then repeated on a daily basis. In addition, his main compulsion in life was to be punctual. He made it a habit to always run all of his timepieces ahead by ten minutes. It bothered him that his Blackberry kept correct time. If he could, he would have changed that too.

Every day he prepared his own breakfast and lunch at Mt. Ebal; being careful to eat the same foods that consisted of eggs for breakfast and tuna for lunch. Dinner was, however, special. The Professor often ate super at the Ladiga Inn which was a small restaurant located on the town's square. The unsold paintings of a local artist hung on its walls. A place where social happenings were as important as the fried food they served. He especially enjoyed the predictability of the buffet offerings. Fried catfish and hushpuppies would always be available on Friday evenings while apple pie was served each day of the week.

To avoid having either colleagues or strangers engage him in conversation, he would sit with his back to the main entryway. Every evening the hostess asked him where he would like to be seated; a polite gesture considering that everyone that worked or ate at the Ladiga Inn with any degree of regularity knew which booth was his. It was reserved by the establishment like that special church pew that no one dared sit in except for the chosen few. He demanded, appreciated and resented the special attention given to him.

Seated inside the restaurant were other university faculty and staff. Some were happily discussing their work while others were there out of loneliness and a need for a balanced, even if fried, meal. An autistic faculty member as well as an unattractive librarian sat alone in their own booths as did the Professor.

Outside on the brick paving stones was his vintage VW Bug. It was parked in his exact spot at the exact time. The oil dripping from his engine marked his spot as reliably as the town dog marked the Confederate monument in the center of the square.

It being Friday, he decided to plan for the weekend as he ate. The weekend was the only exception to his rigidly planned life. No matter how much effort he put into planning for the two days, it never produced the results he hoped for: conformity. What were added to Saturday and Sunday were boredom, loneliness and the heightened awareness of the rapid passage of his life. Each weekend was, like the tick of his hall clock, forced upon him.

- 2 -

THE COLLECTOR

As a collector, he loved to spend as much of his time as possible traveling to various mountain trade days. Near Ladigaville was the longest trade day in the United States lasting for hundreds of miles. Due to his frequent participation, he was starting to have a fine collection of early Alabama artifacts. He could always rationalize that this was a part of his quest to know more about the State's history and to use such knowledge in his classes.

Yet it was the backwoods, remote trade days that interested him the most. They offered selections that had not been picked over by the Atlanta shoppers hoping to find a Renoir hidden behind the primitive painting of a barn. The five senses were needed to truly experience a trade day of the kind that he most enjoyed. The vibrant colors of a primitive painting excited him; the dialect of a valley enthralled him; the feel of hand-carved and polished wood comforted him, while honeysuckle and primrose added wild scents unknown to those who lived in nearby Atlanta and Birmingham.

It was a beautiful fall day when the Professor decided to take a ride in his VW convertible. The air felt cool as he rode with the vent windows open and the top down. Before him the fields bore myriad colors of reds from changing leaves and the yellows of blooming goldenrods. An early frost had just started to turn the forest leaves, effectively reducing the bothersome pollen. Beneath each bridge that he crossed, clear waters roared loudly, having received nourishment from the early fall rains.

He drove miles that day under a sky of brilliant cobalt blue. He was so happy to be on the open county roads he didn't even notice the time, direction or distance traveled. Since he lived near to two different state lines, it was not uncommon for him to venture, often unaware, into western Georgia or the southern edge of Tennessee.

As he drove, he regretted having drunk so much coffee. He knew better than to consume more than one cup before leaving the house on a drive. His bladder soon began to rule his thoughts. He now recognized that it was necessary for him to look for a place to stop.

As he drove over a bridge, he noticed a place ahead to pull off where the shoulder was just wide enough for him to park. He exited the car and started to unzip his trousers when a small dachshund appeared from the dark adjoining woods. The dog looked starved and even smaller than its breed dictated. It crawled towards him as one would humbly before a saint, then backed away. Feeling sorry for the small dog, he entered his car to get a piece of a pimento cheese sandwich he was willing to share with the apparently abandoned little dachshund.

When he reemerged, the dog was nowhere to be found. In a moment, he heard a whimper from the dense underbrush. He followed the sound into the forest just long enough to come upon a small cemetery shaded by ancient white oaks. The dates on the tombstones were from the early to mid-1800s. There were no graves later than 1863. It had apparently been abandoned in that year. There were no beer cans or sprayed-on graffiti common to small rural cemeteries that had been left abandoned.

He had never seen such old dates on markers in his travels around north central Alabama. More interestingly, the roots of the ancient trees that grew within the cemetery were slowly moving the stones. The small dog was no longer visible and all was silent except for the rustling leaves in the treetops. A very uneasy feeling came over the Professor forcing him to quickly retreat from the cemetery. He could sense the presence of something in the shadow of leaves; no form but only the perception that someone was standing there in silence. As he reentered the roadway, he placed the sandwich for the emaciated dog on the shoulder of the road and once more started the VW.

As he drove, he wondered why the small animal had been abandoned in a location so far removed from any village or farmhouse. Why had the animal chosen to stay near the cemetery when there was no apparent trash left behind by visitors? Lastly the main question was why had the small dog wanted him to find the burial site of the long dead?

As his car began to descend from a small ridge that abruptly appeared in the road, he noticed a large homemade sign surrounded by blue, red and white balloons. It read LOST GRAVES TRADE DAY. The lane leading off the county road to the event appeared to be unpaved and narrow but he felt like exploring it.

On the corner of the turnoff, there was a large two-story earthen-toned brick building that was, based on the faded sign painted upon its outer wall, last used as a general store. In its time, it must have been a very ornate building. Though apparently abandoned, there were stained white curtains stirring in the afternoon breeze that extended beyond the windowsills.

As he turned to follow the path, he promised to himself that he would not drive too far along an unpaved road he was not familiar with even if it appeared to be well traveled. Unlike most dirt roads, this one had wagon tracks as well as the imprint of horses' hoofs in the red clay.

The sound of his car quickly echoed from the darkening woods. Occasionally he would pass over a one-lane wooden bridge that rocked and creaked beneath the weight of his car. He soon found himself driving further than he had intended to. Just as he was about to turn around in a pasture, he saw wooden shingled roofs of several farmhouses that were close together. It was obvious that this was a rural community bonded by a common culture. There was not a sign that indicated he was entering a town. The Professor also noticed that there was no water tower for the senior class to paint even though there was a small Depression-era school of unpainted wood. As he passed by, no one on the house porches waved at him nor did the children in the schoolyard acknowledge his arrival.

Then he saw what appeared to be several wagons with teams of mules hitched in close proximity to various vendor tents. Having parked his car under a large white oak that wisteria was slowly strangling, the Professor noticed an aged vendor sitting outside the entryway to his stall. His face was emotionless yet his eyes followed him with apparent interest.

As the Professor walked passed, he saw what he thought was a mannequin propped in the back of the vendor's temporary dwelling. The Professor had previously toyed with the idea of placing such an object in his house to appear as a person. This would, when accompanied by an obsolescent black and white TV set, cause a potential vandal or thief to think that someone was home. In addition sometime in the future, he would eventually install an alarm system. He reasoned that a decoy, TV and alarm system would discourage trespassers while he was teaching night classes on campus. It was also the product of his unease in remaining the sole occupant of the house however temporary.

He had been experiencing the unnerving feeling that someone was watching him both enter and leave the gates of Mt. Ebal. Perhaps it was just images within his own mind that frightened him. He felt, however, that soon a potential intruder would muster the courage to break in and steal whatever he might find. While the Professor did not have expensive tools, coin collections or guns, he did have a new stereo system, a laptop containing his files and a collection of antique books that he valued above all else.

The mannequin was dressed in a water-stained blue and orange gown, holding a book with a marker in it. Strangely, she wore a Venetian mask that appeared to be carved into the frame of the object. Around and upon the greenish blue mask were small red stones, obviously costume jewelry. For a moment, he thought that she could be wearing a discarded evening gown from the 1800s. At a distance, he had at first reasoned that the object was the vendor's granddaughter. Her eyes, like the seller's, were emotionless, but they did not follow him as his did.

Strangely, she wore a Venetian mask
that appeared to be carved into the frame of the object.

The Professor, embarrassed and eager to leave, stopped as the vendor motioned him closer and said, "I noticed you staring at my friend."

The Professor responded, "No, sorry. Just walking past."

The vendor motioned him closer. "Everyone needs a silent partner. I am old and tired. I think I will give up on trade days. No one wants to buy anything. They just want to get out of the house, drive and look around. Everything that I have is for sale, even my partner." He gestured towards the mannequin.

"How much do you want for it?" the Professor quietly questioned.

"Oh, a hundred will do," replied the vendor as he smiled.

"No, I am sorry, that is way too much. Besides, I don't know what I would do with it if I bought it," replied the Professor attempting to conceal the untruthfulness of his statement. He did not want to mention that a growing unease far beyond the loss of material things was the true motivator.

"Sir, I will tell you what makes her valuable," said the vendor. "That mask of hers is part of the wooden frame but the stones. Yes, the stones, they might even be rubies for all I know. Never had a jeweler look at them. Should have. She is probably a hundred or more years old. Her frame is made of hand-carved cypress. The eyes are real ivory and the under wraps are made of fine China silk. I figure that the rough handwoven outer garment was put on her just to keep people from stealing the mannequin even if it is the length of a formal gown. Of course, whoever heard of a southern woman wearing anything like that – gaudy colors and all? I guess it might be some kind of a wedding dress. You know, the kind that a hooker might wear."

"Of course, it might be a gown worn at the Mobile Mardi Gras," replied the Professor. "I once saw a painting in a very old book about the history of Mobile. There was a ball; I think the year was 1857. A woman in the artwork was wearing a mask and a dress similar to that."

"Well, I don't know about that kind of thing," replied the vendor.

"You see, the Mobile Mardi Gras is the oldest carnival in the United States. It is even older than the one in New Orleans. In fact, it started in 1703." The Professor moved closer to look at the mannequin. "What interests me the most is that she is wearing a full Venetian-style mask. I have never seen one like that before. Usually they do not hide so much of the face. The color of her skin just above and below the mask would imply that she is perhaps a mulatto or a person from the south of Spain. Valencia, I would say. It could be, however, that the material has darkened with age. Her blue eyes do confuse me for they contrast with the color of her skin."

"You sure do know your art and history. I never learned much from a book. I don't really care for paintings or traveling."

The Professor replied, "They say that for a painting to be good, it must capture both the souls of the artist and the subject."

"What if she ain't got a soul? What then?" replied the vendor with a quizzical chuckled.

"We all have souls, or at least I hope so. I mean, of course, an object doesn't."

"Are you here to buy her or just look at her?" asked the vendor. "You know, she ain't been stolen since she is so damn ugly. No one has expressed an interest in buying her until you. I thought about taking the dress off and throwing it away in order that people could see the fine wood construction underneath, but then she would not have enough on." He smiled as he changed the subject. "No telling how old the book is that she has in her hand. You know, its binding is real genuine leather. You can tell by the smell. They stopped using that kind of leather years ago. The cheap leather that they used later would just disintegrate in your hand. I guess I had better stop talking, or I will not sell her at any price," he said with a laugh.

The Professor commented, "You mentioned a wedding dress. That is an interesting idea, but I don't expect it will hold up under further scrutiny. It does resemble one in cut, I will admit, except for the colors. It looks like the colors were chosen by Matisse."

"What are you saying? I don't know any Matisse around here."

The Professor, realizing that he was in fact talking only to himself, said, "Oh, I am sorry. I often converse with myself when making historical observations or buying something expensive such as a car. I didn't mean to confuse you. I was talking about the French artist, Henri Matisse."

"I never heard of him," replied the vendor.

"It is not important. Please accept the apology of a senile professor who has taken far too much of your time." After pausing, he continued, "I assume that the original owner is deceased, judging from the age of the material and the fact that it is so water stained. You often see wedding dresses for sale at trade days. It always makes me sad." He paused again. "I noticed that the book in her hand does indeed have a leather binding. To me, that in itself makes it a collectible. Doesn't the book have a copyright or printing date? I'm surprised you haven't checked to see what it is about," said the Professor. "You know that will tell you about how old the mannequin actually is."

"Well, sir, I tried to remove the book from her hand, but the binding started to rip. I guess the hand was fashioned to hold that book in place. Maybe the wooden hand has swelled over time. I don't know anything about cypress. I used to hunt geese in a swamp just north of Mobile before the War. It seems like it was full of virgin cypress." He paused. "Probably, nothing to the book; maybe one of those old German hymnals you can get for under a dollar. No need to destroy it," he said, patiently offering more explanation than he had intended.

"By the way, what do you want with it? Got a store?" the vendor asked. "I may have already asked you that. It seems like I can't remember shit."

"No sir, I have a house in the country. I am away a lot, so I thought I'd have a mannequin sit in the house to make it look like someone is there all the time. Since its joints appear to be flexible, I could seat it in front of the old TV set I have in storage. From the back, she looks very real and is, in fact I think, life-size," the Professor said as he looked the mannequin over once again, sure that it was suitable for the use he intended. "I wonder if the hair is real? It looks like it is." He also noticed for the first time, a wine-colored stain on the right breast.

Neither participant was totally convinced that the answer given by the Professor was adequate to explain such a purchase. Perhaps he should have indicated he was going to give it as a gift to a daughter he did not have. He was beginning to feel guilty for the time and effort that the vendor had taken in telling him about the object. He had, therefore, in effect talked himself into the purchase. The Professor had come to believe his own verbal reasoning.

After writing a check that he promised would not bounce, the object was purchased. He felt very awkward at that moment as he loaded it into his car while being closely observed by the vendor who only smiled as he wrote down the Professor's license plate number in case the check did in fact bounce.

Many of the trade day vendors had dogs for sale. There were bluetick coonhounds, beagles, Labradors and other hunting dogs. Most of them were crossbreeds with unusual coats and odd-shaped jaw structures. The body of the dog might look like one breed while the leg height indicated that it was, in all probability, a mix. The Professor doubted if any of the animals had true papers defining their breed and current status with the American Kennel Club. As the Professor slowly drove past them, the animals growled or barked loudly while pulling on their chains. He assumed that they wanted to join in a collective chase of his VW bug.

The Professor said softly to himself, "I wonder if the dachshund that I saw earlier at the burial ground could have come from Lost Graves? After all, there is a large selection of dogs here."

As he motored past, he was nervous that some of the other vendors and buyers might notice his odd purchase. He had covered a portion of the mannequin with the well-worn tweed sports coat he wore on all occasions, but much of it remained visible as the mannequin was tilted on its side in the backseat.

As he entered the county road by the general store, the car bounced over an uneven portion of the pavement and the mannequin jolted into an upright position. It startled him when he first looked into his rearview mirror. It appeared so lifelike that he felt compelled to say, "Good afternoon, I hope you enjoy your new home." An odd feeling began to emerge within him. He felt as though he was not taking her to his home, but to hers.

After arriving at Mt. Ebal, the Professor was careful not to bang his purchase against the railings of the bannisters that led to the double doors of the entryway. At one point, however, the mannequin's face did hit the door, resulting in a small scratch on the mask of carved cypress wood. "Sorry about that, my dear," he said with a laugh.

- 3 -

COMPANY OF A STRANGER

Daily, the Professor would observe the mannequin as he worked on his mundane research data. He began to notice that the mannequin would occasionally be in a slightly different position upon his return from campus. He knew, however, that he had trouble remembering where his keys were located, so he just accepted its slight position changes as being related to his frequent bouts of forgetfulness.

Daily, the mannequin sat before the TV set. Its reception showed only silhouettes of people moving in black and white snow. Regardless of how he turned it, the rabbit ears continued to provide inadequate reception.

It was Friday night and the Professor had trouble falling asleep. He had built an unnecessary fire only to watch the flames and the sparks that ascended into the flue. Soon he was asleep only to awaken in a dream. Before him was Mobile. He was standing on a wharf as a steamboat blew its whistle at those who had congregated on the dock to watch its arrival. There were beautiful women in hoop skirts and tall bearded men in top hats and coats with tails. It was as though they had been waiting for special guests aboard the steamer to join them. Suddenly, they all waved towards the riverboat.

Then the Professor was standing in a sweet-scented garden awaiting the arrival of a person or for an announcement of great importance. At first, he did not know what he was waiting for. He knew that the South would succeed at some point and that he had already obtained an appointment to West Point. He was home on leave, and he wanted to be certain that every moment was spent in the arms of his love.

Then before him appeared a beautiful young woman dressed in an orange and blue gown. She had been reading for in her hand was a small leather book.

"Anna, I want you to know how much I love you." At that moment they both stared at one another and then embraced. She did not remove the Venetian mask she wore for soon they would be joining the Mardi Gras parade.

"My good sir. I must call you 'sir' for soon you will be my handsome lieutenant."

"Anna, my sweet, I am troubled like all of my friends at West Point. If the South succeeds and it will, I will resign my commission in order that I might serve the Confederacy in uniform." He paused and looked into her eyes. "I want us to be married as soon as possible and for you to joint me at Mt. Ebal. It is far to the north in Lafette County. I know the house is much smaller than your Rose Hill. However, for your safety, the war is unlikely to ever reach there and you, my love, will be safe."

"My sir, are you ordering me to marry you or to simply evacuate to the north of Alabama?"

"Yes, do consider my order to be an expression of a love that cannot die."

"Then pick me a white magnolia bloom and place it in my hand as a token of your love."

The Professor awoke from his dream. Stale smoke from the fireplace filled his study. In the air was the scent of magnolia.

He looked towards the mannequin. "Anna," said the Professor, "I hope that you don't object to our lack of television reception out here in the country." He paused for a moment. "Why?" he thought to himself. "Did I just call the inanimate object 'Anna'? Was the dream a reality?" He searched his thoughts, trying to remember if there had ever been an Anna in his life. He remembered from the distant past having dated an 'Amie,' but had never loved her. "*Anna* and *Amie* are not even remotely similar," he reasoned out loud. "Oh well." He smiled. "*Anna* will do fine. I guess that it is better than referring to you as *it*."

ი

After returning from the university later in the week, the professor began to wonder if what he had written the night before had also been changed during the day. First the textual alterations had been barely perceptible. The tense of a verb might be altered. His written expressions seemed increasingly to be more from a previous time of authorship. In some cases, the word "thou" had replaced a more common pronoun. As an undergraduate, he had taken courses in Victorian and Elizabethan literature. Though he regarded it to be only literature, the *King James Bible* remained his favorite translation of the original Greek and Aramaic texts. Perhaps he was using words read years before as a student. He had received a master's degree in Irish Studies from Boston College before completing his doctoral degree at the University of Pittsburg. His family traced its origin to the west coast of Ireland. The Professor's grandmother, Mary DeBurgo, had often told him ghost stories that were inevitably set in Ireland. Stories that involved fairies – mythical beings whose actions were often the catalyst for terrible events.

Possibly it was just fatigue, but the sentences seemed to have been altered without his direct intervention. Maybe it was just another sign of forgetfulness. Perchance the too frequent jiggers of bourbon enjoyed during his nights of loneliness were having an unintended effect upon his memory. "Maybe I should start drinking more red wine. That's supposed to help prevent dementia, my most dreaded of fears," he mumbled to himself.

The mannequin sat quietly in the room. Meaningless eyes fixed upon the snowy silhouettes. He began to think that the vendor had dressed her in some old, used clothing that had not sold in the store. The Professor reasoned that the vendor's stories of age, cypress wood and ivory were just sales pitches. How else could one explain the water-stained scarf and soiled dress? The clothes were so out of place that they could not possibly have been sold even to the mountain people who held firmly to their fundamentalism and, therefore, shunned gaudy colors.

෪

In the twilight of early evening when he would return from the campus, he would often notice a dark object along the driveway that blended into the woods. He assumed that it was a cedar growing among the pine thickets that had caught his attention. As the summer began its journey into fall, the object was no longer there. He reasoned that since the sunlight must be at a different angle, its disappearance coincided with the changing of the season.

During the last week in October, however, it reappeared. Each evening, thereafter, when he could remember to look, the dark object would be in a slightly different location along the wooded drive. Since he was tired, and the time of day was always twilight when he arrived home, he did not want to stop his car in order to walk into the woods to just look upon a cedar tree or perhaps the trunk of a tree that had died. Besides, wild blackberry vines, now leafless, covered the sides of the road and beyond them, were the young pine and hardwood saplings in various sizes.

He also knew that thorns would pierce his thin suit pants. In that ticks that dwelt in the woods about his home had often bitten him, Lyme disease was an ongoing concern that he could not erase from his thoughts. He had already been very sick with the disease and now feared that arthritis would be the unwelcome guest of his past illness.

The winter too quickly followed the vibrant colors of fall. The crisp cool air that he enjoyed was soon turned into the bitter cold breath of winter. Ice formed upon the garden pool's waters and silence gripped the landscape. The migratory birds no longer journeyed to the wetlands of the Gulf. The streams flowed less rapidly having become choked with autumn leaves and the quiet slush of ice.

The isolation of the winter intensified his feeling of being alone. The heater in the Professor's car was not sufficient to make his leisurely drives in the countryside comfortable enough to enjoy. His only pleasures were reading and looking at the color of the light as it made patterns across the bindings of his leather-bound books. The music of Chopin accompanied him into the late hours of the night.

He loved the sounds, colors and odors of the roaring fire. As the ashes deepened in the hearth, he enjoyed stirring them to generate new heat and abundant sparks. The voice of the wind within the chimney shouted loudly on winter nights, stirring even more the embers that soon died as he slept upright in his well-worn leather chair.

He often spoke to the motionless inanimate object. His make-believe relationship with her began to bother him. Often, the Professor carried on a conversation with Anna interspersed with songs recalled from the church hymns he memorized in his youth, a punctuation of the silence that became more profound with the passing of each winter day.

If he could speak so bluntly and honestly to both wood and fabric, why not to a living person? Did he not inwardly desire the warmth of a human's presence, desire's fulfillment even if it were only in a touch?

He still noticed the young coeds in his classes and the radiant graduate assistant, Roxanne. She would occasionally smile at him but few words other than professional courtesies were ever exchanged. She was beautiful and fully aware of the fact. Roxanne was boldly flirtatious with other members of the department but not with him.

"I am not even forty. What is wrong with me that no one desires my presence?" he said to Anna.

Yet there was some comfort even in his isolation. Due to the wide selection at the recently renovated university cafeteria where he ate when he had an early afternoon class, his meals were prepared to his liking. His punctuality was assisted by the mechanical-like service of the staff. He felt at times that he was trapped by autism that demanded a rigid schedule that had to be followed at all cost, including his desire for companionship and love. His military punctuality and rigidity were essential to his life creating an island of individuality.

The selection of his CDs did not vary. Occasionally, he would find classical music at ridiculously low prices that he would add to his growing collection. Chopin performed by unknown Eastern European orchestras. He also loved "Prelude No. 1" by Bach. His very favorite, however, was "Reverie" by Debussy. Even his choice of music isolated him from the more progressive on campus who preferred what he considered the deafening rapping of metal upon metal.

"Anna, perhaps it is best that I am alone except for you. My agreeable and consistent companion."

Rather than a Microsoft announcement of events, his antiquated wooden tickler box filled with non-alphabetized index cards with frayed yellow edges reminded him of each of his appointments. The Professor was painfully aware that he was growing more isolated through his habits. He had become his worse academic and social critic.

- 4 -
SEASON OF CHANGE

Soon rain turned into the tapping of sleet upon the metal roof. The floors now felt inordinately cold when walking barefoot from room to room. He loved to tread barefoot for the texture of wood felt good to him. The rougher the heart of the pine boards, the more soothing they felt.

He could never find his house shoes even if he made a point of leaving them in a particular location the night before. He knew that soon he would become the classical professor – forgetful and alone in a smoke-filled room.

The snow arrived late in the year making its appearance at the very beginning of February. February in the Deep South was often a month of extreme contrast. Snow followed by rapidly rising temperatures, then pursued by a few warm days was the typical weather pattern of the southern Appalachians that year. Just warm enough for the peach trees to bloom and then for the promised fruit to die from frost. The tornado-plagued month of March was still far enough away.

&#x03;

After the snow ended and the promise of the warmer days returned, the nights intensified the Professor's emotions. He, like Ingmar Bergman's Professor Isak Borg, thought of the failed opportunities, the mismatched relationships. As he drank more, he remembered that he had never attempted to look at the book Anna clinched so tightly in her hand nor noted the page carefully bookmarked by a dangling piece of yellowed cloth. "Who cares?" he thought. "Probably like the vendor said, a Lutheran hymnal or something else useless or he would have reclaimed it." When the Professor tried to take it from her hand, the grip was so tight that the book could not be removed. Obviously the mannequin had been exposed to enough heat or decay to cause the object to have become permanently gripped. Yet he would stare at it wondering what it possessed within its frozen pages.

With the ending of February and the promise of an early spring, he looked forward to his return to Mt. Ebal each day after work. Upon opening the door, he knew he would be greeted by the scents of life. The house would be filled with the smell of honeysuckle and wisteria, and so he waited.

ೞ

Birds flocked to the small pond in the garden area while carpenter bees sought fresh wood to bore holes within. The fruit tree blossoms had yielded to small, green, hard buds of expectant fruit. The nearby forest of cedar, white oak, sweet gum, dogwood and pine yielded a rich background odor. The dogwoods bloomed in the radiant color of pure white.

The house, in the daylight, was a most pleasant place. Far from the worries and responsibilities of his administrative and academic duties, it fit his need to be alone and in company with the mountain's beauty. "Am I the only one who sees the gifts nature bestows upon the southern Appalachian Mountains?" he asked Anna.

The frequent afternoon thunderstorms were an extra bonus to the sensual delights offered by the mountains. Lightning would strike the nearby mountaintop yielding a display not seen in the city. The bolts would not only travel to the ground but also dance horizontally to adjacent low clouds – thunder being the product of their mating. The ozone would quickly arrive providing a fresh, invigorating odor stirring the mix of early spring Appalachian mountain smells. This was a house of contentment, loneliness and yet increasing unease.

His oak desk had been bought at an antiquated drug store that sold a collection of unrelated items. Easter cards still lined the upper shelves intermixed with Christmas cards. The customers were seekers who believed that under the next pile of unsold clothes, various cardboard items and out-of-date magazines, there was a van Gogh to be found. The desk was the only wooden one for sale among a collection of Korean War metal desks that had been purchased by the proprietor for later resale. The Professor bought the wooden desk for thirty-five dollars and thought at the time that he had paid too much.

He liked the desk. The fact that it was dark rough wood attracted him. The scratches, dents and chipped surfaces indicated that a life had at one time been present in its use. He loved wood because he could work with it using tools purchased at various trade days. Soon he had fashioned a bookcase from pine that he placed on its desktop, a bookcase he never managed to varnish for he loved the natural sight of aging wood and the breath of pine. A swivel chair, from an old Texas general store owned by his great uncle, provided the finishing touch to the somewhat physically uncomfortable but eclectic collection.

As he read his notes in preparation for the next day's class, he kept looking at the coarse fabric that constituted the mannequin's outer garment. The stitching had become very loose around Anna's shoulder, revealing a silk-like material underneath. Drink in hand, he arose from his chair and walked over to take a closer look. Beneath the stitching, he could see the off-white fabric of the mannequin's skin.

The garments were obviously very old. He touched the shoulder and ran his hand down its length. The outer material was very delicate. Some fibers were left clinging to his fingers. It was apparent to him that the cloth had not been handmade on an early Alabama loom. How old would the dress have been?

"Based on her choice of colors, it is obvious she represents a woman of the upper class. At first I associated her with poverty only because I purchased her at the trade day. How foolish of me, a historian, to not have been aware of that.

"No wonder the garments have been placed on the mannequin, they are without any value due to the shedding of fiber – useless in a synthetic-prone world. The stains will be impossible to remove due to the age of the garment."

- 5 -

Ms. Webster

The day had been long. Students lingered in the hall after his final class had been dismissed, asking questions designed to impress the Professor.

After the other students had left for the evening, Natalie, a graduate student with short brown hair, continued to capture his attention. "Professor, I want you to know that I find mature men attractive, especially the intellectual types. You know, the ones that are odd but brilliant, the flaky kind."

The Professor looked into her eyes and then at the floor tiles. "Ms. Webster, I think there may be a compliment in your words. Think carefully of what you are saying."

"Professor, I prepared a gift for you." She handed him a small box that had been taped shut.

"Ms. Webster, I don't think it is appropriate for me to accept a gift from one of my students," he said while looking closely at her lips. As he dropped his stare, he looked for the briefest of moments at her breasts and then quickly his eyes traveled down her body to the floor.

"It is considered impolite in the South not to accept a gift once offered. Besides, I noticed that you just looked me over. I hope you liked what you saw," she said with a smile.

He paused unable to clearly communicate. "Ms. Webster..."

"Professor, please called me Natalie. Every man needs a temptress. I am yours."

"Ms. Webster, I mean Natalie, I am a full professor with a career that I truly love. Would you have me risk it for a moment of pleasure? I am not a person that considers affairs of the heart to be only, as you would call it, free love."

She took his other hand and directed it to her breast. There it remained. "Now, Professor, that you are under my spell, open the box."

He could not believe that he was responding physically to her aggressiveness, his hand now cupping her breast. Suddenly from the faculty office came the piercing ring of his phone. He withdrew his hand, placing the box upon his desk, and quickly walked to pickup the receiver. "Hello," he said. There was no immediate response. "Hello, anybody there? Hello! Hello!" There was no reply. Suddenly the phone uttered only the dial tone. When he returned to the hall, it was empty.

The Professor stood there silent. He walked down the rows of empty classrooms and then opened the exit staircase door. There were no sounds in the building.

He opened the box. Within it were photographs of Natalie. She was posed nude in various positions on a period fainting couch. It was obviously the work of a professional photographer since the images were lit by strobes and floodlights and the props were well made. He had seen the shops of such photographers in Gatlinburg, Tennessee. Many of who often specialized in Civil War settings for those willing to pay the cost.

The Professor looked very carefully at each of the three photographs of Natalie. Then he came to a forth image. It was the print of a woman in what was perhaps a multicolored gown from the mid-1800s. The facial skin, partly covered by a mask, was too poorly lit and out of focus to allow him to determine the ethnicity of the subject. Also, the dim light of the image prohibited him from being able to see the detail of the dress. It was obviously a reprint from a very old photograph or perhaps even that of a painting. He could not tell. Its presence contrasted intensely with the erotic images of Natalie.

He walked to the dean's office and immediately shredded all of the other photographs except of the woman in the gown. As he destroyed them, his hands trembled. Never before had he felt so disgusted by his own actions. "To think that I touched a student.

Impossible! Impossible!" he said out loud to the quietness that surrounded him. "I will ask Natalie about the last photograph when I see her again in class. I am sure she did not intend to include it in her solicitous collection of images."

As he went back to his own office to heat up one last cup of burnt coffee before leaving for home, his cell phone rang. "Who could that be?" he asked. "It is almost ten in the evening. Could it be Natalie? Surely not! Perhaps a student who had forgotten her purse or a cell phone in the room? Worse yet, a charitable organization seeking more donations. Damn them for calling so often!" He lifted the receiver to his ear. The Professor's cell phone was an old model with poor reception. Whenever he answered a call, he often heard static noises emanating from it. He shouted, "Hello! Hello!"

"Are you coming home?" a young woman with a heavy Southern accent asked. It was a voice he had never heard before.

"Madam, I am sorry but you have the wrong number!"

The caller insisted once more, "Are you coming home?"

Convinced the repeated question was harassment and being, after all, very tired, he ended the call by pressing his finger forcefully on the off button. Immediately, he wished he had noticed the caller's number. He had no way of knowing the number since he had discarded the instruction booklet years ago and did not know how to retrieve the information.

"What could I have done if more had transpired? A threat, perhaps? Call campus security? Yes, that is what I will do. I will not be harassed."

CB

He stepped outside of the Education building. The night was windy with rapidly moving clouds that played a child's game with the moon. He had expected, perhaps hoped, that Natalie would be standing there, waiting for him. He could not see anyone under the campus lights that lined Trustees Circle – the lights ran throughout the university campus designed to ensure the safety of students while intensifying the darkness of isolated areas.

When he arrived at Mt. Ebal, the porch light was on just as he had left it. An owl sounded nearby. The sky was clear and the stars seemed very close and bright. He loved the shadow of trees cast by the full moon. Some of the stars now radiated their vivid colors. He heard an animal moving rapidly through the adjoining woods. "Damn the interruptions! I should have been home hours ago."

He fumbled for his keys, dropping them onto the wooden porch floor with a loud thump. He thought to himself that, after all of the years he had owned Mt. Ebal, he would finally be able to figure out which key was the correct one. Instead he fumbled with different keys trying to make each one fit.

The low-watt porch light was very dim and his night vision was not good. The dim light was the source of frequent irritation. He uttered out loud to the night wind, "Damn it, when I have enough time I will replace that fucking bulb!" A distant dog barked, then silence ensued. Even the owl had stopped creating its usual auditory effect of intensified isolation.

He remembered the strange photographs a friend had taken of the house that revealed orbs of light in the yard, invisible to all except the camera lens. Perhaps he now stood within such a circle of light or one might linger nearby unseen by him. Legends, he knew, told the listener that the orbs of light, when seen in the dark forests of Europe or upon the English moor, were the souls of those who were doomed to roam the earth in search of a love that had been lost or denied to them.

The spheres of light, however, to more critical minds were relegated to only dust on the camera lens and so were easily dismissed without further investigation. However, upon closer examination, the orbs that surrounded Mt. Ebal contained a unique image that was not representative of the myriad patterns of other natural phenomena such as snowflakes. The orbs appeared to contain some form of rudimentary protoplasm. Each orb was similar yet possessed its own unique biological code similar to DNA. Mt. Ebal was, therefore, a house surrounded by circles of unexplainable light. Some large, some small, some close, some remote, others touching the earth while many appeared to rise into the night sky like smoke being emitted from many chimney flues.

As he entered the parlor, he spoke jokingly to Anna. To him, she had lost her inanimate status. "Must have been you calling. Thanks for checking on me." Anna sat before the TV set while silhouettes in static continued to move upon the screen. Her soulless expression remained constant. "Guess it wasn't you after all."

Having poured himself a drink, he sat at his desk, searched for unpaid and now lost bills and stared at the mannequin. Nearby was the landline phone necessary for his dial-up modem. He didn't remember placing the phone on the table close to the television. Oh well, he couldn't find his socks most mornings even when leaving them at a specific spot on the highboy the night before.

To him, Anna represented his relationship with others. His lack of involvement demonstrated his uncaring attitude. He too had become lifeless and without emotions. Her meaningless stare was the reflected image of the Professor's soul. Perhaps behind the mask, was something beautiful, a smile or a knowing glance? He acknowledged the impossibility of revealing her facial features, yet he longed to know who or what she truly was.

ೞ

He thought back to an encounter at another university. He had traveled to south Alabama to attend a professional conference involving international distance education. His university hoped to establish a relationship with a Chinese institution in central China.

The conference invitees were seated at several tables for an evening meal and presentation. The Professor had arrived late and found a place next to a younger gentleman. When the Professor sat down without saying a word, the stranger arose and left. Then a very attractive blonde woman asked if the seat was available. At first, he hesitated, unsure whether its former occupant was going to return or not. He then looked into her blue eyes. "Yes, of course, please be seated." It was not long before they were involved in conversation for they shared several interests including hauntings. The Professor mentioned that the house he owned was very unusual indeed. The hours passed rapidly as they discussed the probability of an actual haunting.

"Robin, if a presence exists, then it verifies the existence of the soul."

"Professor, if that is the case, then the search for a haunting is noble if not foolish."

"Regrettably," he replied, "it provides verification only to an individual. Only one can witness a visitation if he lives alone as I do. There needs to be another person present to serve as a witness."

"Regardless, a person who has seen and believed has been most fortunate beyond all others," she replied smiling.

Questions came to him in rapid succession. Why then had he sought the company of a stranger? Why had he been so bold at a conference to share such intimate thoughts that at best must have seemed bizarre? Why had she accepted his invitation to see the images of the house in his hotel room? Why had he asked her to spend the night with him?

Then suddenly, he thought back to the evening's phone call. A thought that bothered him was the static noise he heard in the background whilst speaking to the unknown caller. The television static now sounded eerily similar to what he had heard earlier at the university. "I must be very tired to even think about such a pointless coincidence."

"One thing I know for sure is that you didn't call," he expressed once again out loud to both himself and Anna as though seeking her reassurance. Anna's face possessed only a frozen emotion. The faded red lips on the mask did not move nor did the pupils contract within her deeply recessed eyes.

He felt restless even though it was nearing midnight. The Professor had placed his desktop computer in an adjoining room on a cheaply purchased desk. He preferred his laptop for many tasks, but still enjoyed the feel of his older desktop computer. The monitor was large and the keyboard was ergonomically correct.

He heard distant thunder that signaled a storm was fast approaching Mt. Ebal. As he sat waiting for his computer to load data, the room lit up as lightning struck nearby. The explosion of thunder immediately followed, the sound like cannons firing. He did not have time to recoil as the room became instantly dark. He was disorientated. The Professor reached for his flashlight. Instead, his hand touched his camera. He rose from his chair and walked towards the center of the room, then tripped on some books he had carelessly stacked on the floor. "Damn it! Damn it!" he shouted in the darkness.

It then dawned on him that he had better sit down. "I will use the camera flash to orient myself." The flash went off immediately lighting the room. His hand continued to touch the shutter resulting in multiple flashes. This allowed him to miss the additional books he had carelessly tossed on the floor and find his way back to his desk safely. The storm soon ended and the power was restored. Since the flashes were for illumination only, he did not think anymore about the images he had taken.

ᴄȣ

He arrived early at work the next day. After attending a morning Academic Council meeting during which he deleted nonessential e-mails on his Blackberry, he walked across the campus to his office. The meeting had lasted far too long in an endless dialogue of trivial matters, and he had paid the price for having drunk too much coffee. He was thankful when the meeting ended. His mitral valve loudly protested his inordinate consumption.

As he hurried back to his office, the large oaks and tall pines provided a perfect shade for strolling about the campus. A sweet smell from the bushes that lined the walkways pleased him. At a distance, he noticed a coed walking in the same direction he was headed. From the back, her size, the black hair draped over her right shoulder as well as her overall appearance seemed very familiar. She was clothed in a long dark dress clutching what he assumed to be a textbook. "Must be one of my students. I just wish I could remember names," he thought as they both walked in the same direction, the distance separating them did not decrease even though he quickened his pace. Soon she rounded the edge of the College of Education building. For a brief moment, her side profile was discernible. It seemed impossible, but to him, it appeared to be that of Anna's. He hesitated as though his leg muscle had frozen. "It must be the distance. My eyes are very tired from reading so many reports."

"No, it is not possible!" Thoughts came to him in a random fashion as he walked quickly towards the spot where he had last seen her. To him he was attempting to justify the personification of a mere object made of cypress. The Professor increased his pace to reach the edge of the building. When he arrived, only an empty tree-lined sidewalk greeted his stare. "She must have entered the Education building," he said to himself. "No point in going in to look for an illusion. I need to get back to my office."

ೞ

He had noticed that he had grown more anxious about so many things. He remembered how his father, also a professor, had taken his ungraded papers to an erosion site on the family farm used for dumping, or as his father referred to it, "for filing." He thought for just a brief moment about disposing his ungraded papers in a similar fashion. "No, I am too professional. That is my problem."

"Perhaps I drunk too many vodkas last night," he reasoned. He needed to talk to a friend that could understand the complexity of his thoughts and experiences. He could not admit any weakness to his colleagues. Certainly not one that suggested he might be hallucinating. Such a rumor could exile him to one of those remote offices on the third floor of the administration building intended for those who had tenure, had become old, bitter or forgetful, and for whom the organization feared a lawsuit might result from their too obvious dismissal. "Age discrimination, that is what it is called," he thought to himself. The administration building, because of its date of construction, was not required by federal law to have an elevator. This fact was not lost on the university's budget-conscious administration.

The Professor looked forward to his evening class. He wanted to ask Natalie more about the images she had given him, especially the picture of the woman in a ball gown. In spite of his efforts, he could not forget the images of her on the fainting couch.

Before the class ended he said, "Ms. Webster, I would like to talk with you after class." She acknowledged his request with a smile.

Once the last student had departed from the room, he turned towards her, "Natalie, I mean Ms. Webster, I wanted to talk to you about our last class meeting. You handed me a small box with photographs in it."

"Professor, I am sorry, but you must have me confused with another student. I didn't hand you anything after our last class."

"Ms. Webster, I remember distinctly your having handed me a small dark-colored box that contained four images. Three of the images were of you, and the forth was of a woman in a mid-nineteenth century ball gown."

"Professor, I am sorry, but I did not hand you anything. Why would I give you photographs of myself? It is true that I wore a ball gown two years ago. It was a KA dance at the fraternity house. You know it is a Southern fraternity that has a yearly ball. Everyone dresses in period costumes, but I would not share any pictures of my gown with a professor or any other stranger."

The Professor looked at her sternly. "I don't want to argue with you, but you did give me a box with photographs in it. I am only interested in one picture. That of the woman in the ball gown."

"Professor, if that is true, show me the photographs."

"Well, Ms. Webster, I shredded the ones of you."

"What?" asked Natalie. "If they existed, why would you have shredded them?"

"Well, to be honest and blunt, you were nude in them."

Natalie looked at him and laughed. "You are really flattering yourself. There is no way on earth I would share something like that with someone I'm not romantically involved with. Did you keep the one of me in the ball gown? If so, show it to me!"

"Yes, I did keep it, but it is not a photograph of you. It may be a photograph of a painting or a person. I just can't tell."

"Professor, I know that I am only a student and that you have a lot of control over my future, but let me suggest that you visit the campus infirmary and ask for a referral to a psychiatrist." With her words, she turned and quickly went down the exit stairwell. He heard the door close heavily behind her.

og

As was his habit, he returned to his office before heading home. Having left the pot on for much of the day, he could use a strong cup of coffee. He added two spoonsful of sugar and further masked the burned flavor with his favorite artificial non-dairy creamer. "Well, I know where I put the image. It is right on my desk. I will make a copy of it and share it with her the next time we have class."

As he stirred the coffee, he decided to look at some digital pictures he had taken earlier of a uniquely beautiful woodpecker. Its bright red head and black-and-white body promised to yield beautiful images. The bird had visited Mt. Ebal on several previous occasions to feast upon the insects in a dead oak tree whose decaying trunk bordered on the deep woods that surrounded the house.

He was very pleased with the many shots he had taken earlier of the bird. At the end of the nature sequence, he advanced without thinking to the next image. It was the one he had taken during the power outage caused by the storm.

At first glance, he noted a fog encroaching upon the room from the bottom of a closed window. Even though it was his practice to always keep the window slightly open regardless of the season of the year, he had lowered it at the first sound of thunder.

In addition, instead of the camera being directed towards the desk that held his computer, the camera images were taken facing an easterly direction – the same direction from which the fog had appeared. He clearly remembered pointing the camera in a different direction before taking the photograph or at least he thought so. Perhaps his orientation had been confused when he stumbled over the books he had careless lain on the floor.

The next frame showed the vaporous image increasing in size as it also did in the following frame. It still appeared to be entering the room from the bottom portion of the window. The last frame showed it extending from the floor to above the ceiling fan blades.

"What on earth?" said the Professor as he connected the camera to the USB port on his office computer. Enlarged before his eyes, he saw the phantom image fill the 20-inch screen.

The Professor immediately advanced to the next image. Instead of an image of the room, it was a digital picture of television snow. The next image after that was the same. He did not recall ever taking a photograph of the black-and-white television screen in front of the mannequin. While studying the image in detail, he thought, "Why would I ever take a picture of that?" A feeling that he expressed out loud in the empty room.

At first, he considered showing the images to his friend in the history department. Then he reconsidered. "If this gets out that I am the least bit interested in the paranormal, my reputation as a scholar will be in question. What benefit would there be in it for me if I showed the whole world such nondescript photographs? The majority of people would think I altered it."

After relaying frightening dreams that proved to be visionary, his mother had warned him as a young person that he might be what she described as a portal between the living and the dead. He inwardly knew that he needed to fight against his natural instinct to be sensitive to dark places and antique mirrors. He strove to avoid even a cursory discussion of the supernatural. He resented the fact that he was being swept into a world that he had so desperately sought to avoid.

In all the years that he had lived in old houses in the country, he had never seen a fog enter a room and form a shape in the middle of it. It had occurred to him that the only other explanation had to involve the camera. Perhaps it was defective. Then he remembered that he had just previously taken some excellent images of the woodpecker in the yard. In scanning those pictures again, they appeared to be perfectly clear of any camera-induced defects.

Then he thought, "Perhaps if I show the images of Mt. Ebal and my Texas farmhouse to a priest, he might help me understand what is happening. I have not been to a confession in years. I do remember, however, the name of a priest in Baton Rouge that I might be able to talk to. I will send the images to him as well as some of the disturbing photographs of my childhood home in Texas. It is possible that he will be able to offer some sort of learned explanation that might shed additional information on the subject. I hope I can find time to do this in the near future."

Up to this point, the Professor had forgotten about the challenge that Natalie had presented to him, that of showing her the image of herself in the ball gown. He looked about his desk. There, turned upside down before him, was a photograph. He took it in his hand and glanced at the other side. The picture was totally in black as though ruined in development. "My god! My god! What is going on?"

He remembered the remark he had earlier made to a friend when first considering the purchase of the Mt. Ebal: "If a spirit dwells within the house, it will verify the existence of either good or evil." The thought had earlier intrigued him. But now, he said out loud to the silent room, "Am I to be punished for my disbelief?" His confidence was now replaced by fear.

- 6 -

THE WARMING

Driving in rural Alabama, in the warming of the season, continued to be one of the Professor's favorite pastimes. He remembered his very pleasant drive to Lost Graves. He thought about the narrow paved roads that always led to hollows and small towns. He loved to talk to vendors along the sides of the winding road. Wildflowers added to the aroma of the occasions. He continued to look forward to the Saturday yard sales that wainscoted the main streets of rural towns. Often with a glass of sweet tea with lemon in hand or a jigger of bourbon from the glove compartment, he enjoyed spending Saturdays in his VW bug driving casually among the hills.

As he approached a long stretch of vacant road, a nondescript, rusty black 1960s pickup truck began to pass him. He thought nothing of it and moved his vehicle to the side of the road as both cars approached the bridge over a rapidly flowing stream. As his vehicle moved nearer to the inadequate guardrail, the truck drifted into his lane forcing him closer and closer to the embankment. He honked and rapidly considered his alternatives. When the truck sped up, he attempted to swerve back into his original lane after forcefully hitting his brakes. As the truck began to pass him, the driver slowed down by his window. Behind the dark-tinted glass, the passenger looked straight ahead, emotionless. Then she slowly turned her head towards him. In that moment the truck increased speed, leaving him behind to regain control of his car. He swerved just in time to avoid hitting the guardrail and plunging into the rapidly flowing waters below. "No, it can't be. No, it can't be," he thought. "My imagination has become my reality!"

After crossing the iron bridge, the Professor pulled to the edge of the embankment, his heart pounding in his ears. He looked down the road in order to see more details of the truck. Since he always carried binoculars in his glove compartment, he hoped to get the license plate number. There was, however, no automobile on the road that he could see even with the powerful lenses. The sound of cicadas grew louder as did the sound of running water that fed the nearby stream.

ॳ

That night, he returned to Mt. Ebal. Instead of reading, as was his usual habit, he went to bed early. He lay there in silence going over the events of the last two weeks. Had he worked too hard? Perhaps his eyesight was failing? Was this an indicator of heart disease? Was he going mad? With each thought, he turned in bed. He attempted to think about pleasant memories but nothing worked. He kept returning to the emotionless face in the pickup truck window. After a brief moment with his eyes closed, he then suddenly opened them wide to see a round circle of light between his bed and the wall. The circle appeared to contain protoplasm within it.

A few weeks earlier, another colleague, having heard about the orbs, had wanted to photograph the yard at night using a digital camera and flash. The second set of images yielded surprising results. He recalled how the orbs were everywhere around the house and that they tended to concentrate around the front bedroom area – the room he was now sleeping in.

"What a coincidence," thought the Professor. "This is the room where a former tenant had died and where my mother had her premonition of approaching danger." The object that at first had appeared stationary began to move about the room. With awakening fear, he jumped to his feet and cut on the room's light switch. Instantly, it was filled with light from the incandescent bulb. No object was there. "Have I been sleepwalking?" he thought. "Could it have been simply rogue light from the road? Impossible."

The next night, he once again tossed in bed, repositioned his pillow and tossed some more. Soon, however, he found himself asleep. A vivid dream immediately appeared in which he was seated opposite a person in a straight back wooden chair. The room was dark except for what appeared to be key lights directed at him and the individual directly across the room from him. The stare of the stranger was piercing in its intensity. His clothing was from an era he did not recognize, perhaps European. His face was drawn taut. His features were like a line drawing in shades of gray similar to an image in which hatch marks yielded both perspective and shadow. He appeared like one that had never enjoyed the warm sun or had bothered to gather the delicate flowers of the bottom woods in youth or experienced the beginning of love.

He noticed in his own hand his father's revolver, an antique black Navy-issued .38 pistol. It felt heavy and cold. In the other person's hand was a similar weapon. Neither pointed their gun. Instead they both let it dangle from their fingers.

The guest said, "I am he that has been written of. If you kill me, you will live, but your soul will be with me forever. If you fail to fire, I will kill you instead. Do you have the faith to die now?"

With all of the Professor's doubt and immense fear of the void that would surely follow his death, he tightened his grip on the gun, but could not pull the trigger – one more sign of his failure to commit to anything or anyone.

The dream ended in the blast of a single shot but only a sound within the dream and nothing more. The Professor awoke sweating. In his hand, now trembling, was the revolver from the dream. In his sleep, he must have opened the nightstand next to him and gotten the gun. A gun that he always kept loaded. What had awakened him was that his head was resting uncomfortably upon the barrel. His index finger was wrapped tightly around the trigger. The dream had become reality. Had he shot the presence, he would have killed himself. Anyone investigating the scene would assume it was an apparent suicide of a deeply depressed man. After all, a person alone without friends or family had sparse reasons for living.

Morning twilight was now filling the room while the shadows shifted into form. Dark morning clouds floated upon the sea of the awakening red sky. The orange-tinted full moon began to lose its brilliance. The Professor placed his feet on the cold pine floor and remained for a moment silent.

- 7 -
RETURN TO THE VILLAGE

"Perhaps I should return to the village where I purchased the mannequin. It seems like many of my concerns started after I bought it. Maybe if I asked the vendor some additional questions, it might help. He can tell me about any unusual circumstances that occurred regarding the object such as might have happened to him or could have been passed on by its former owner," he reasoned as he drove to his office having made numerous stops behind a school bus. Those pauses in his drive gave him time to think about the dream and the other events that had transpired at Mt. Ebal.

At work he asked a geography professor who had lived his entire life in Lafette County where Lost Graves was surely located. His friend replied, "You have got me. I have never heard of a Lost Graves in this county. I imagine you drove further than you thought; maybe even into Georgia. Are you sure 'Lost Graves' is the name of the town?"

The Professor replied, "No, I am not sure of anything except the events of the day. There was no city sign, only the trade day announcement that I assumed was the name of the town. If I try, maybe I can find it again. I wish, however, that I could tell you the county road number, but I cannot remember it. I don't even recall seeing a road sign. At the time, I just wasn't interested. I just wanted to enjoy the day."

ॐ

The next Saturday, the Professor loaded his ice chest into the car and two ready-made sandwiches he had earlier bought at a Cowboys convenience store. He thought he could remember the route he had taken, but he was not completely sure. He didn't remember crossing into Georgia, but it could indeed be a possibility. He did not use maps on his drives. He wanted them to be completely spontaneous, free of any intent except that of pleasure.

Like before, the day was beautiful. He cut on his CD player and listened to New Age music that soon soothed him.

An hour, then two passed as he drove. He knew he would never be able to find Lost Graves again unless he completely relaxed in order to enjoy the beauty of the moment as he had done previously. Perhaps inwardly, he did not want to find the town since that would imply a purpose to the trip. The car reached the summit of a rise and then began to descend just as it had several weeks before. He had somehow found the exact location he had been searching for. "This isn't possible," he reasoned. "No one has this kind of luck – good or bad."

The trade day sign was no longer visible but the general store was right where he remembered it being. Instead of drapes flowing from the upstairs rooms, only broken glass suspended in decayed window frames could be seen. As he drove closer, it was apparent that the roof had long since collapsed onto the bottom floor. No longer was the store name visible, having been removed by the flaking off of its paint.

"What on earth?" thought the Professor. "This surely is the same store, but it is now in ruins. Maybe I didn't observe it well enough last time." Then he made the turn onto the road that ran alongside the store just as he had done before. Instead of finding it well traveled, grass grew in the center of the lane and tractor tire imprints were all that told him that it had been recently traveled upon. He then backed up onto the country road he had just left.

"This is a mistake, yet the building is the same one I saw previously. Perhaps if I drive on down the county road some more, I will find someone who can tell me about the building and the trade day event that I attended," he reasoned.

Near the abandoned store was a two-story farmhouse that was unpainted but obviously well lived in. "The occupants should be able to tell me something about the trade day," he reasoned. He could not, however, imagine why he had not previously seen the house. Perhaps the large trees had hidden it in their shadows.

He stopped in front of the dwelling and stared at it from the perspective of a historian. The house was from the antebellum period with formal balance even if one of the eight small columns that supported the front porch was missing resulting in the sagging of the hipped-style porch roof.

The dentil molding above the windows was of high refinement indicating that a prosperous planter had at one time occupied the structure. Instead of formal gardens, the yard was now scraped-clean as had been the tradition of poor Southern families during the Great Depression. Chickens in the yard necessitated that the Professor watch his steps carefully in order not track their waste as he walked towards the front door.

Just as he stepped onto the porch, a large dog came from behind the side of the house with its ears back and teeth bared. It did not bark but was silent in its approach. The Professor's heart pounded for he had an unexplainable phobia of dogs.

"What you doing here, fellow?" said a faceless voice from within the dark wide hallway. "Back, Jake, back boy!"

The large dog sat down immediately on the porch while pointing itself directly at the Professor's leg, its ears now reared in obedience; listening for the next command.

"Sir, I was at a trade day several days ago at Lost Graves. I remember turning down the road by the general store to get to it. Now, there seems not to be much of a road at all. Can you tell me when the next trade day will be?"

"What ya talking about? Where did you hear about Lost Graves? You a drinker?" said the person from the shadows.

"No, sir. Only occasionally and definitely not while I am driving." He could not believe he was responding so politely to such a rude and personal question.

"Well, there ain't been no trade day at Lost Graves since I was born. In fact there ain't no town down there anymore."

"Sir, I realize there is no town there, but I clearly remember several houses and a trade day. In fact, there was even a school," replied the Professor.

"No. You don't remember shit. The only thing down that road is the cemetery where all the people is buried," replied the voice.

"What do you mean, 'Where they are all buried'?"

"Are you questioning me?" replied the unknown person in a strong localized accent.

"No, sir," answered the Professor defensively.

"There was a big storm came through here over a hundred and fifty years ago that started over somewheres around Lafette County or maybe Saint Claire County, only the Lord knows for sure. It went right through Maggie Hills. That was the name of it then. Destroyed the churches, school, people's houses and killed nearly all the ones living in them. It happened on Palm Sunday or so my great grandmother wrote in her journal. They were having a celebration that day after church, and they was all together in the meeting hall. I think that word had been received of a victory for our forces over around Chances Creek. Maybe, if I recall correctly, one girl from Maggie Hills, my great grandmother wrote, survived and she weren't right in the head afterwards. Maybe the young girl weren't here at the time but somewheres else when the tornado hit. Maybe over in Lafette or Cherokee county. I probably have the whole damn thing wrong. Can't remember nothin' these days. Doc said that she had a brain swelling. I think that they later put her away in Tuscaloosa because no one could handle her."

"Do you know her name?" asked the Professor, alarmed.

"Nope. Now wait, maybe it was Alice, Anna, Alicia or something that started with an *A*. Can't remember clearly," replied the faceless voice.

The unknown person walked down the darkened hall and shut a hallway door loudly behind him. The Professor was now left alone on the porch with the dog. He knew he would obtain no further reliable information from the person in the hallway. He slowly walked down the steps and then hurried, without running, to his car. By then, the dog had risen to its full height. Ears pulled back, it growled and moved aggressively towards him. The Professor knew no one would be there to call the dog back now. Thankful to be inside the Bug, he quickly rolled up his windows as the large animal pressed its fangs against the driver's side glass. Its wide jaws quickly began tearing the canvas top.

ଔ

He thought it would be interesting to drive down the road as far as he could go to see if what he had been told was correct. As he turned at the general store, he surveyed the destruction of the store where age alone had been augmented by the unrelenting cycle of heat, rain and freezing cold. Some faint spray-painted graffiti remained on the walls.

He drove down the road and entered the thickening pine forest. Soon the road approached the iron bridge he remembered crossing. He stopped, abruptly noticing that the wooden floor of the bridge was missing. Under it, a stream flowed with a strong current that created eddies. In the distance, there was an impenetrable forest of old-growth pine trees. The road that had become a trail ended at the foot of the rusty bridge. The Professor knew it would not be too long before it too fell into the stream, the banks having been undercut by the flowing water.

The Professor stood staring, mesmerized by the stream, and then looked towards the woods that prevented his seeing further in the direction of Lost Graves. There was no way he could cross the rapidly flowing stream in order to venture further. Besides, what would he find there?

He then looked at the damaged convertible top. Teeth marks had sunk deep into the canvas.

Perhaps only a psychiatrist or a drink that evening could put him at peace or provide an answer to the impossible. He also noticed the lengthening of the shadows and realized that it would be best to return home before dark since he really did not know where he had been.

The ride back to Mt. Ebal was at first uneventful except for the strong feeling of exhaustion that he had to fight in order to stay awake. Even though he thought that he remembered the way along the winding roads that led to the gate of Mt. Ebal, he found himself lost. Down one darkening road after another he drove until he saw a house that did not look familiar to him. Then he would turn around and repeat the same folly. For what seemed like an hour, he drove aimlessly as though he was in a game where the participant was blindfolded and twirled to the amusement of others.

Finally having arrived safely home, he prepared early for bed and took a hot bath. The rising steam relaxed him, the frustration of having been lost quickly eased away. Afterwards, he retired to his study, drunk the bourbon and water he had poured and placed his head into his hands. The only sound he could hear was the ticking of the clock.

Suddenly, he heard what appeared to be scratching upon the windowpane. The room became very cold and silent. The ticking of the clock stopped.

A frost appeared on the glass followed by a soft taping, like a person using the tip of a finger. Then in horror he watched as letters were being scratched slowly, one at a time, into the thin film of ice that had formed within the frame.

A finger writes upon the pane.
A thought speaks in silent voice.

Now two within a dream appear
The seeker and the sought.

His heart raced as his chest tightened. He could not remove his eyes from the words. Slowly the letters disappeared as the room temperature increased. Outside only moonlight could be seen as a night bird flew from the magnolia tree, loudly flapping its wings. Then only the clock ticking in the hall was heard.

cos

He refrained from the stigma of seeking professional help and the bourbon offered at most only temporary relief. Something kept bothering him the following week. It was a strong feeling that a required action had not been completed. The more he thought about it, the more apparent it became that he needed to go to Tuscaloosa to find out about the girl whose name started with an *A*.

He assumed she must have been admitted to the state institution there and they would possibly have information related to her. Then it dawned on him that privacy laws would prevent the gathering of such information. It also occurred to the Professor that he had an acquaintance in the Criminal Justice Department at the university that might be able to pursue the matter further for him.

The Professor contacted his colleague, "Gordon, would you mind doing me a favor? There was a young girl from Maggie Hills, later known as the Lost Graves community, that was admitted to the state institution in Tuscaloosa. All I know is the first letter of her first name starts with *A*. I know it is not a lot to go on, but she was in a tornado that occurred there in the 1860s. You know, the War years."

Gordon replied, "You don't have anything more than that? That is not going to help a great deal. The only thing going for us is that she was from Maggie Hills or as you said later, Lost Graves."

"You have heard of Maggie Hills and Lost Graves?" questioned the Professor.

"No, that is the good thing. No one else from Maggie Hills would probably have been committed unless there was a problem that was inheritable in her family, and then the family would have taken care of her by asking for state assistance. Maybe I can find a database that list those institutionalized by the town and county they lived in. It is a wild shot, I know, but maybe I can find something for you. I will send you an e-mail if I do. But the time period is also against us.

Remember, there was a war going on at the time and lots of records were destroyed. I am not even sure Tuscaloosa had any facilities to care for people during that time period."

ভ

Four days later, the Professor received a phone call from Gordon. "I'd rather not e-mail you about this, so I thought I would give you a call. First, I asked around and no one had ever heard of Maggie Hills or Lost Graves in either Alabama or Georgia. Everyone assumed I was asking about Maggie Valley in North Carolina. I did find a friend, however, that knew how to access a database that provided the information we needed. The information was not digitized but instead was on microfilm that had been copied from very old handwritten ledgers. By the way, she was from Mobile County not Lafette. How far did you think you had driven? Never mind, you must have driven at least two or three hours. You owe him one for trying to figure out how to load the microfilm reader. I didn't even know those were still around."

Gordon continued, "There was only one person admitted from Maggie Hills, assuming there is only one Maggie Hills. Her name was listed as Alicia Fennegan. I admit that my friend had difficulty in reading the handwriting. He thought, however, that he had copied the name down correctly.

"She was admitted in 1863. The only other information about her was that she was released the same year. I am sorry that I cannot help you more. I imagine that this is probably not the person you had in mind. I tried to find out more about the tornado, but there were no references to it in any source materials that I could locate. Usually, I am pretty good at this type of investigative work. Probably no one kept track of tornadoes in that time period. The Indians knew more about these kinds of storms than the early white settlers, and they in turn left little written history. There are some pictographs that depict tornadoes but they, of course, are not dated. We are not even sure who drew them. There has been no attempt to date them. Besides, it could have been the early white settlers themselves since they were basically illiterate.

"Oh, there is something else you might find interesting. You mentioned you had a connection to Mt. Ebal in northeast Alabama. Mt. Ebal is in the Bible as the mountain where the people were forewarned concerning Biblical curses. In addition, I read that the Indians referred to Mt. Ebal as the Mountain of Evil. The early settlers changed the name to Mt. Ebal since they had trouble with the accent of the early Indian traders that dealt directly with the fur trade. Just a history lesson that I thought you would be interested in. Let me know if I can be of further help."

Back in the solitude of his faculty office, the Professor reasoned, "How could it be possible that a man out in the country could have known about the one survivor from a tornado that occurred close to two hundred years ago and from a village that no one has even heard of now? The chances of there having been a written diary in that time period is very remote since most of the rural inhabitants could neither read nor write. Perhaps there was a local historian in the community that recorded the event, but I doubt it. Another possibility is that the person I spoke to was descended from the same family as the only known survivor of the community. He could even be a direct descendant of hers. Since she may have been insane, he probably would not have wanted to admit to the relationship."

Upon returning to Mt. Ebal, he noticed that he had received some new e-mails. One of them was from Father O'Dea. He quickly opened the correspondence from the priest. Father O'Dea had forwarded his e-mail to another priest who had performed church-sanctioned exorcisms. He in turn forwarded it to a lady in the church who traveled with him on each of his assigned visits.

According to the e-mail, the priest called upon her whenever he obtained permission from his bishop to perform an exorcism. In addition, the priest would take her with him to do things like praying and to point out areas of special concern. The e-mail further praised her for her gift in locating demonic spirits that required exorcism.

Upon seeing the images, the assistant had responded:

Regarding the pictures of the two houses that you sent to Father O'Dea, there is something very bothersome about them. My experience teaches me that things are not always what they appear to be. God always reveals a great deal more when I arrive at a site.

The farmhouse is the more troubled of the two houses. It appears that witchcraft or sorcery has occurred. Something happened there that allowed unusual spiritual activity to take place. I feel that it is haunted by a soul that is not at rest.

There has been abuse and violence in the farmhouse, possibly someone was killed within its walls. The soul must be prayed for in order for it to be released. Demonic spirits are there because of the violent events that occurred.

Mt. Ebal shows that witchcraft or sorcery may have been practiced by a previous occupant. The house shows that it has been affected by occult activity. The result is that there were left openings for the demonic to enter and continue to be present. The chimney, the right room and window have something troubling about them.

Without prayer and cleansing, the two houses should not be occupied. I fear for anyone that now lives within them.

The Professor did not know what to make out of the correspondence. Was Father O'Dea suggesting that both of the homes that he owned needed to be cleansed through separate exorcisms? He further noted that the priest himself had not mentioned any particular photograph, but instead had relied upon both the opinion and recommendation of a most unusual woman, Mrs. Ruth Spencer. Perhaps the Professor would choose to think further on this at a more convenient time.

It did bother him that Mrs. Spencer had referred to the right facing room and the windowpane. This particular windowpane was directly in front of the mannequin. "Had the psychic been able to peer into the darkened room?" he questioned.

- 8 -

THE MANUSCRIPT

Robin had earlier written to the Professor in that they shared a common interest in creative writing. The Professor had a passion for writing short verses that were not of publishable quality. He would, however, occasionally send a poem to her since she was also on the editorial board of an avant-garde printing house.

Out of courtesy, he thought, she previously suggested that a collection of his poems might indeed be publishable. In addition, he had sent her the outline of a book he planned on writing later. The book dealt with the antebellum house that he both loved and feared, Mt. Ebal.

He often sought insight into himself within the verses that he wrote. Perhaps revealing more than he intended, the next day he penned:

Thoughts on Returning to Mt. Ebal

Who am I keeping out with gate and chain?
The wind does not acknowledge my privacy
nor fire keeps its distance.
That which enters is not invited
but lingers, explores, penetrates.

Friends do not venture near so posted a place

nor strangers knock upon the door.
Have welcomes ceased and friends become intruders?
What do I own: this hill, this wood, this meadow?

I am the intruder on land forbidden.
What I seek is not here nor will I find it in mansion or ruin.
Your smile, your touch; only thoughts linger,
explore, penetrate upon this spring-touched summit.

When Robin returned from a trip to Slovenia where she had traveled for a non-profit group, she sent him an e-mail:

"I am working on formatting and preparing your book. I enjoyed reading the somewhat lengthy manuscript. The illustrations were very interesting and will lend themselves to furthering the narrative."

The Professor had only submitted a short collection of free verse poems and an outline for a possible future novel. He certainly had not provided enough material for the contents of a novel, much less one involved with a haunting.

The supernatural had never been of interest to the very practical Professor. It was true, however that he had jotted down an outline related to the unusual happenings in the house. It was only an outline for a possible story, an outline he did not intend to share with anyone except Robin. He didn't intend to publish a book about the house or the Confederate camp located nearby.

Yet, Robin's e-mail implied that she had received a completed manuscript with illustrations that he assumed might be architectural rendering. After further deliberation, he thought, "How can this be? What could possibly be in such a manuscript and, more importantly, who sent it? Perhaps Robin has confused my book outline with another would-be author's desire to publish a book dealing with early Alabama history."

He relayed his concern, through a text, to Robin who commented that it would be better for her to meet with him in person rather than discuss the draft over the phone or through e-mail. She stated that it exceeded the standard e-mail file size in that it contained a great many full-colored illustrations. She indicated that she found the manuscript to be complete and, in her opinion, publishable and wanted to address some formatting issues with him in person. In addition, there was a contract to be negotiated. He said out loud to himself, "Has she not been listening? I did not send her a completed manuscript!"

In an earlier e-mail, he had in fact proposed that they meet at Mt. Ebal. The purpose of such a meeting was to write about the house and the historical events that had transpired there. He felt that if they discussed the various happenings, then they could work as co-authors in publishing an interesting book that combined both history and romantic adventure. As a result of her initial rejection of such an idea, he had not pursued the matter further.

- 9 -

JOURNEY

Robin realized that she had made a hasty decision to go to Mt. Ebal. Her son had called at the last moment, saying he was held up by his business and would not be able to visit with her. Since the cancellation occurred so late, she was unable to get an inexpensive flight to Atlanta. Unwilling to drive alone, she decided to take Amtrak. She did not want to spend the money on a sleeper, which she considered unnecessary spending, but instead chose to ride in the passenger car occupied by what one traveler referred to as the living dead – people exhausted from jobs in factories and malls visiting those that did not care to see them.

After boarding at a dimly lit station, which opened only thirty minutes before a train's arrival, in the suburbs of Washington D. C., she looked about her. There were only four passengers in the railcar in which she rode. Three of who were already sleeping, having eaten ready-made sandwiches. They had, for economic reasons, refused the porter's suggestion of pillows that were offered at a nominal charge. Their heads now rested at various angles like jointed marionettes at rest. The fourth person appeared to be an elderly woman who was looking straight ahead and failed to make eye contact with her.

Robin looked forward to the opportunity to eat alone in the dining car. In her youth, she had ridden to various states with her grandmother who had free railroad passes since her grandfather had been a conductor on the Santé Fe line. Sleeping cars were not included on railway passes. She had taken several long trips to Missouri, Los Angeles and Chicago. Robin had always found the passengers to be more interesting than the scenery.

The train car moved through the dark night. It shifted from side to side, dependent upon the condition of the rails and the degree of the curves. Upon entering the dining room, Robin was required to be seated by the porter even though all of the tables were unoccupied. She was soon escorted to her table.

Standing in the threshold of the entryway was the older woman she had previously noted in her train coach. Her hair was in a bun that exposed the wrinkles on her neck. Her dress, once lavender, was now a faded color, the hem reaching just below her knees. Her mismatched garters held her torn hosiery in place.

Robin thought, "Please don't let her be seated near me."

The porter led the woman directly to the vacant chair across Robin. The uninvited guest grasped the tabletop and let herself fall into the seat. At first, she failed to make eye contact with Robin.

"How are you doing?" asked Robin out of respect for her age.

The woman did not reply but stared instead at the menu placed before her. She circled her choices and waited for the waiter. She then looked at Robin.

"You are going to Alabama, aren't you?" she said softly.

"Why, yes, ma'am, I am," Robin replied.

"I know. I can always tell where someone is going," the uninvited stranger said.

"Where are you going?" Robin inquired.

"To New Orleans," she replied and stared at Robin.

"Oh, I am so sorry about all the damage caused by the hurricane. It must have been terrible. Is that your home or are you visiting there?" Robin spoke almost apologetically.

"It is my home. I have lived there all of my eighty-three years. I will die there as well," she said.

"Oh, it must be nice to know your future," Robin replied uneasily.

"Yes. I know my future and others' as well," the woman said as she adjusted the napkin in her lap.

"Do you have the gift of prophecy?" Robin asked.

"Everything is written."

"I don't understand. Written where?"

"You will know when you get to the Appalachians," the stranger replied.

"Pardon me," said Robin with a sense of unease. "What is your name?"

"My name is Nettee. My mother was a mestizo and my father, French," she replied. "Being able to read the future is a gift I inherited from my mother's people."

Robin responded, "I have never before talked to a person that could read the future. I don't think I want to know what will occur tomorrow or even tonight, much less years from now. I think that some things are best not known." Robin continued to feel uneasy yet curious. She knew that no one possessed mystical powers. She thought it odd in this century that anyone would want to listen to such fantasies. It was true, however, that people would pay to feel good or be entertained.

The meal was eaten in silence except for an occasionally pleasantry. The world outside the dining car did not exist. The reflections of the night were but images from within the car itself. Occasionally the train would pass a flashing stop. Car lights that penetrated the reflections could be seen lined up, impatiently waiting for the train to pass.

When Nettee finished her meal, she excused herself from the table and reentered the passenger car.

As the train moved through the rural and darkened countryside, Robin kept feeling that Nettee, who was seated several seats behind, was staring at her. It was the uncomfortable feeling she would get during a church service when a man would glare at her. Nearly always, she would meet his eyes, then smile and look away.

As the train slowed at a terminal near the South Carolina border, Nettee rose, reached for her cardboard-like luggage and walked, falteringly due to the movement of the slowing train, towards the exit door. Once abreast Robin, the train's abrupt halting jolt stopped her progression. Nettee's face, under the passenger car lights, appeared wrinkled, her eyes yellow and bloodshot from lack of sleep or possibly from concern. She spoke in a strong New Orleans' accent. "Don't go to the mountain. Don't go! There is no good to be found. Only lost graves are there." She then moved towards the front of the car in order to disembark. Robin felt concerned but did not attempt to seek any additional explanation from her as the conductor motioned her to leave the train car.

"Why was she getting off so soon?" thought Robin. "New Orleans is still a day away."

- 10 -

TRAIN STATION

The Professor spent the day cleaning the house. It was a truism that old homes quickly replaced any dust or cobwebs that were removed by broom or dust rag. Odors returned like the cold air's breath beneath a winter's door.

He considered whether he should put Anna in the caboose behind the house, or simply leave her in the same position he had become so familiar with. Would his guest understand the mannequin's original purpose or would she think of it as an object of contempt, purchased at a Peachtree Street sex shop in Atlanta? He then decided that he would alter nothing. Why hide himself from the very person he wished to communicate so freely with? He gathered honeysuckle, baby's breath and mountain roses. The Professor placed them in an antique vase on the crudely made table fashioned from a past storm's debris.

ఴ

The day seemed far too long. Meetings followed by two lectures from notes brittle to the touch. Finally, he was on the highway to Atlanta. His thoughts were interrupted by the unusually heavy traffic that caused a mild anxiety that he might not arrive on time. All of his life, he had been the first to arrive and the last to leave. He knew that the secret to any success he had known in life could be attributed to his punctuality. In his classes, he referred to it as "The One-Hour Rule of Success." When he discussed it on the first day of each class, students yawned and smiled at one another; that is, those that were not busily texting their lovers.

As he faced the oncoming Atlantic traffic under a rising moon that was beginning to be cloaked in rapidly moving clouds, he thought of what had transpired in his life that had led him to this awkward moment. He knew that Anna must be a product of his own self-imposed isolation from any meaningful relationships.

How could he love again when the storm a few years before had destroyed all the objects of his affection? He knew too well that the mannequin was only intensifying his unease about a future that was to be spent alone.

"Perhaps Anna is only my conscience restlessly stirring within me." The Professor thought back to a quote from James Dennis Carroll, "Conscience is no more than the dead speaking to us."

Why then had he sought the company of a stranger? Why had he been so bold at a conference to share such intimate thoughts that at best must have seemed bizarre? Why had she accepted his invitation to see the images of a house?

After a discussion of past events that were only meaningful to him, he had asked her to spend the night. "Yes, only to be rejected," he earlier had said to Anna.

Now, he relived their meeting in the solitude of his car. They had met at a conference in Troy, Alabama. When arriving for the prepaid meal, he was seated next to a faculty member that shook hands with him and then remained silent. Without explanation, the faculty member got up from the table, without excusing himself, and went to another nearby table where he once again sat in silence. First ill at ease thinking that the relocation had something to do with him personally, the Professor was pleasantly surprised by the arrival of a late attendee at the conference. She sat down next to him, ordered her meal and smiled. She told him that her name was Robin and she was an associate dean at a university in upstate New York. Their conversation involved their creative writing efforts as well as their mutual love for historical homes.

The traffic slowed as he neared Atlanta. Pulsating arteries of traffic approached him. He continued to think about his future guest and the purpose of her visit. Was he beginning to be infatuated with Robin even though he did not know her except through their mutual love of poetry, historical houses, and the awkward moments spent in Troy?

Were his needs so great that a brief meeting and later correspondence could translate into such emotions? No, he had to concentrate on the events that had formulated their meeting and yet he wondered. He knew that emptiness creates a void to be filled with the force of an ocean's swell that enters a rocky crevasse but does not remain.

The Professor left his car with a parking service and rode MARTA to the train station holding tightly to the safety bars as the bus driver sped past slower cars. Even though he had mapped the train station on his computer, his limited night vision and nerves would not allow him to mingle with the Atlanta traffic. There, strangers from around the world were to briefly stare at him and then continue their discussions in languages far remote from the Deep South from which his culture had originated. A land of failed crops baked by August suns, allegiances to lost causes, and an unshakable faith in divine purpose. A land in which even a child's death was justified by an eternal plan: "It is God's will."

It was not unusual for relatives to photograph their dead children in coffins placed upright in the yard in order to get enough light to properly expose the images. Such events were to be expected and recorded. He knew that the rural language, while not grammatically correct, still communicated ideas both clearly and succinctly if the intended recipient was from the South. He also understood that *everything works for good for those that love the Lord.*

His mind wandered like that of Leopold Bloom's in James Joyce's *Ulysses.* "Would she be there?" he wondered.

His cell phone rang loudly. The caller asked, "When will you be home?" The Professor's hand trembled and the phone dropped to the hard bus floor spinning on its axis. He did not recognize the voice that now frightened him. It sounded too much like the caller from the other night when he was on campus. He knelt to pick the cell phone up, his hands trembling. Not having time to check the number from which the call was made, he swiftly debarked from the bus upon its arrival and stood alone on the sidewalk. Thick fog, the product of a nearby reservoir, shrouded him.

- 11 -

ARRIVAL

The air was very cold when Robin stepped from the train. The fog had greeted her on the deserted walkway that led from her railcar to the station. She retrieved her bags from the porter, tipped him, then waited inside the terminal. The building was much smaller than she had imagined considering the large city where it was located. Like everywhere throughout the United States, the stations she had visited were largely vacant buildings located in the deteriorating urban landscapes.

The Professor had deliberately failed to mention that she could have ridden all the way to Anniston, Alabama rather than disembarking in Atlanta. He didn't mind picking her up in Atlanta since it would give them a two-hour opportunity in the car to get to know one another.

She exited the station briefly to see if he might be waiting outside. The station was empty of passengers and the ticket attendant could be heard speaking to another person in an interior office but did not emerge to greet the new arrival. As she reentered the night air, she noticed an older woman walking down the ramp that paralleled the tracks. The stranger soon disappeared into the thickening fog. "That woman seems familiar to me," Robin thought. "Of course, I don't know anyone in Georgia, especially not an elderly person." Still it bothered her that the woman resembled a person she knew. "Perhaps I will recall whom she reminds me of later."

Out of the fog from the other direction appeared the Professor. She assumed that it was he as she waved. He was wearing an overcoat and a hat that looked like a 1930s stage prop borrowed from a university drama department.

Then his eyes saw her. Trembling, he extended his hand to greet her in a far too formal manner. Robin Finch's blue eyes smiled warmly at his greeting. He did not want to stare, but in a brief moment, he captured her entire body in his mind. She was real!

"Robin, I really appreciate your coming to Mt. Ebal. This is certainly an exciting opportunity for us to explore and write about a series of most unusual happenings," he said.

She responded, "Professor, I am really anxious for us to talk. Your manuscript certainly surprised me. I didn't expect it to be so well written. It requires virtually no editing. The illustrations included certainly add to the plot. You are, by the way, an excellent artist. I can't believe you failed to mention that to me in your e-mails."

"Robin," he interrupted, "I didn't send you a manuscript, only the outline of some events that I thought might be of interest and that we might want to write about later. I doubt I provided you with more than three or four pages of brief descriptions that involve a series of inexplicable happenings at Mt. Ebal. I do think, however, that you will find what happened at Mt. Ebal very interesting. It is certainly a house with a colorful history. As you may have read on the Internet posting, it is a structure that refuses to be destroyed."

Rather than returning on MARTA, he hailed a taxi. The noise and jerky motion of the cab, as it raced across the city streets, precluded any meaningful conversation. Robin noticed the contrast between the beautiful buildings and the congregations of drug addicts and gangs that stared at them from adjacent corners at each red light.

Upon arriving at his automobile, the Professor opened her car door and held it until she was seated. He then adjusted his rearview mirror. The traffic was lighter than usual, and soon they found themselves endeavoring to depart Atlanta on Interstate 20. Few words were spoken as he attempted to find an up-ramp to the interstate.

Robin continued their earlier conversation, "I am very interested to hear more about Mt. Ebal. I can sense there are several additional stories you would like to relate."

"Please don't let me bore you. As I mentioned previously, you might find the various incidents of some interest. After all, we still have several miles to drive." He asked, out of courtesy, "Are you sure you want to hear about Mt. Ebal now? I know you must be tired."

"No, please. That is one reason why I have journeyed here," she said with convincing sincerity. "Your additional e-mails regarding the house fascinated me." He was somewhat surprised by her comment, considering that her replies to his few e-mails had been only a few fragment sentences long.

"There is so much to tell. Let me begin with an almost trivial happening. The spring had been beautiful followed by the warm air of summer. The branches of the large rose bush in front of the house were filled with buds and mature roses. The corn had been planted neatly in many rows and bore tassels as we anxiously anticipated a crop of roasting ears, a justification for the work and expense of purchasing a tiller. The thoughts of corn in large pots, salted and buttered, accompanied by baked chicken on a warm, still Sunday afternoon created excitement. My childhood memories of hot apple pie following the Sunday meal were recreated.

"One day upon our arrival at the top of the hill, upon which both the corn and the house sat, the corn laid scattered in all directions. It was as though a small storm or whirlwind had singled out the corn for destruction. Each stalk had sustained enough energy to force the strong-rooted base from the red soil. Upon close inspection of the recently tilled earth, no marks of an intruder could be seen. No other sections of the garden suffered such an occurrence nor a review of the potted plants, that sat upon the porch, or the rose bush indicated the presences of a strong wind, much less one of such force as to uproot the corn. I wish now that I had reacted to my instinct that something was amiss in this small display of nature's fury. A force that would later climax into the destruction of the house and the alteration of my life."

"It must have been a dirt devil. Isn't that what you call them in the South?"

"Yes," replied the Professor, "you are correct."

They both exchanged relaxed glances as he concluded the brief conversation. She found him to be much older than she remembered. His eyes reflected the emotions he had earlier expressed regarding the house: determined, analytical, disturbing, piercing.

His intermittent smile reflected an unhappy early life. The Professor's childhood had been lonely in the large, rural Victorian house of tall ceilings and dark wood. He was not allowed to have friends visit. Soon the house and the objects within it had become his playmates – living objects of ancient wood and iron his only companions.

☙

The road soon became wet and slippery which forced the Professor to slow down to an uncomfortable speed. He quickly found the Heflin, Alabama exit then proceeded down a two-lane road that was deserted of any traffic.

His headlights highlighted three people walking on the side of the road. Their backs were to them as they approached. Each had a quilt over their head and shoulders in order to protect them from the rain. As a consequence, their features could not be seen. The Professor swerved to miss them, quickly regaining control of the car that had skidded on the rain-slick road.

Robin asked, while trying to regain her composure after the skid, "Isn't it unusual to be walking down a road in the rain at night? It seems very dangerous. They didn't even have an umbrella between them. One of the people looked to me like a woman. It would have been nice if you had offered them a ride."

The Professor's voice changed, "Robin, this a different part of the nation than you are used to. Relatives pickup relatives. They would never have gotten into a car with a stranger even if a woman was present." The Professor did not want to get his car seats wet, but the real answer to his hesitancy was the fear that Anna was one of the three. It frightened him to verbalize his anxiety in his thoughts. He continued relating stories about his Texas home. The sound of the windshield wipers grew louder.

"As I mentioned to you in an earlier e-mail, I have loved my Texas home almost as much as I have loved Mt. Ebal. To me, the two are linked."

Robin spoke loudly as the rain struck the windshield, "Your Texas home? Oh, I forgot you still have a farm in Texas."

"After the installation of the Victorian hall doors at the Texas farmhouse and the placing of the mantelpiece from a Galveston mansion, a progression of unsettling events occurred. My mother took frequent walks in the morning before the Texas sun created ripples of heat upon the road. The road was tree-lined and the favored route for funeral processions between the rural village and Lanora Cemetery, much like Mt. Ebal with its nearby burial ground. It too had been established at the same time as the construction of the house. The road in front of my home was now largely untraveled except for an occasional tractor or truck loaded with wheat. It was my mother's habit to walk the road alone, in the early morning hours, while my father tended to the fields.

"Far down the road, Mother noticed a woman walking towards her. Being accustomed to recognizing people at a distance, she failed to identify the lady as being local. As the woman progressed towards her, it was apparent that she was wearing a brown blouse with similarly colored shorts. Soon, my mother could see her face – a silent face, devoid of feelings often visually expressed when meeting a stranger, revealing little or no emotions. She stared straight ahead and failed to acknowledge my mother's body language, a language accustomed to expressing a warm greeting to a stranger. Instead the woman continued to walk straight towards her with an expressionless stare, unblinking and piercing. Mother thought that surely the woman would speak and so maintained her path. As the woman neared, she did not alter her speed of walking or her direction. At the last moment, my mother gasped as she expected the impact of their bodies. Instead, the woman in brown walked through her and as my mother turned in amazement, the woman continued to walk away from her and soon became indiscernible from the heat mirage now generated by the rock and oil road.

"In great fear, Mother ran towards the farmhouse, finding my father in the backyard, and reported the incident. After first denouncing the event as silly, he walked to the road, looked both directions and saw nothing. The event occurred under a clear sky in daylight. My mother had not consumed alcohol or taken any mind-altering drugs."

The Professor continued, "I asked her if she had ever seen the lady before or after the event. She responded no. My mother, a psychology professor, did have an interest in the occult. My grandmother loved to tell ghost stories to all of us as children. Later, she was to tell Mother not to venture too far into the unknown. She reminded her that any attempt to contact the dead was expressly forbidden by the Bible."

Robin looked at the Professor. "I do believe that some people are more sensitive to the paranormal than others. Perhaps it is an inherited gift." The rain continued as they drove to Mt. Ebal.

The Professor looked again at Robin. "The last incident that I will bore you with prior to our arrival at Mt. Ebal also relates to the farmhouse. As a student, I had studied late into the evening. The house was silent except for night noises that are customary to old country houses. I was alone and had enjoyed my opportunity to explore my subject matter in greater depth. When my eyes began to tire, I climbed upon the four-poster bed filled with contentment that my work was finally done. As I looked towards the tall Victorian doors, I suddenly saw a face. Its eyes were a piercing stare. I jumped from the bed, grabbed my loaded shotgun and pulled the hammer back, prepared to fire. As I started to press the trigger, the face vanished. The room appeared as it had before. The night sounds of the whippoorwills, crickets and coyotes remained as my only companions."

Robin replied, "Both houses seem to have a lot in common. It may be that you subconsciously created such a commonality. Perhaps you are overly sensitive to both houses since you have indicated that they are not just objects of wood, but are living structures."

The Professor did not comment as the car rounded the last turn in the county road that passed in front of Mt. Ebal.

- 12 -

PREMONITION

As they drove through the gate, Robin noticed the steep incline of the rain-streaked concrete drive. The windshield wipers rose and fell rhythmically. The headlights aimed at low hanging clouds while the Professor used the bordering pine trees to maintain both his direction and secure his path. The car stopped and only the splattering rain sounded with occasional thunder in the distance. The house and porch lights were on just as he had left them.

The house was beautiful to her as it appeared in the flashes of lightning. It was like a cave into which a frightened animal would flee without knowing what sat in the impenetrable darkness. The Professor took her luggage and quickly followed her to the porch steps as the rain dampened their hair. Slowly he progressed up the many steps under the weight of three tightly packed suitcases.

Robin stood motionless for a moment on the porch that was supported by four Doric columns and looked towards the peaks of Appalachia's ancient summits. Lightning revealed black clouds and dark forest. The sound of the rain running off the eaves masked other sounds emanating from the darkened wood that surrounded the house on all sides. Cold water dripped from her blond hair and ran down her neck, but she did not notice the chill.

She was happy the trip had ended and she was finally at her journey's end. The lights of the house promised safety from all that she was fleeing – loneliness and self-doubt. It did not matter that light can be a flame that attracts the moth to its own destruction.

The Professor opened the double doors to reveal an interior from another era. It was as though she were stepping into 1850. The air in the house was still. She noticed that a fire had been readied for their arrival for the damp air did offer a chill. She did not notice other parlor details as the Professor led her down the hall to a furnished bedroom.

While all the other rooms were made of horsehair and plaster, the hall walls were constructed of hand-hewed rough wood on which wallpaper had originally been hung. The tongue-in-groove hall walls also appeared more recent, suggesting that the front rooms of the house might have been repositioned from a different time period.

"But why?" the Professor had earlier asked upon purchasing the house. The question was a result of his need for analytical precision. This might also correlate to the carelessly offset doors at both ends of the hall. The juxtaposition of the back hall door and the surrounding walls would accommodate the placement of a very large object in the hall. In all likelihood, the object would have been a coffin since death awaited both old and young. The front portion of the hall ended in the double doors, often referred to as funeral doors in the vernacular of the South, that provided just enough space for the coffin's passage.

He placed the luggage on the wide-planked pine floor of the bedroom. The rain streaked across the windowpanes as a clap of thunder mildly shook the house. She then thought of the Spartan furnishings and asked the Professor, "Have you been living here long? There are so few items of furniture."

"Robin, I really have not had a need to possess more. As you know, the tornado destroyed most of the house, and for a long period of time, I did not want to return. I lost all of the antiques I loved. I found only a fragment of marble from the top of the dresser that I had treasured. As you will note, most of the furniture here now is homemade. If the violent wind returns, it will take only wood and not memories."

Robin looked at the Professor whose face was expressing a degree of sadness as he looked away from her. It was the first time she noticed more than a superficial expression of emotions. "You lost more than possessions in the storm, didn't you?"

He did not answer her question.

The kitchen smelled of spices while the hallway and bedroom were filled with the aroma of myriad wildflowers. Regardless of the wild, primitive scents, the breath of the house remained. Timeless odors oozed from the floors, wardrobes and darkened adjacent rooms. The scents were not unpleasant, but reminded her of her childhood home in rural Oklahoma, a juxtaposition of both happiness and fear.

Robin and the Professor entered the dining room and seated themselves on opposite ends of the handmade dining table. Steam rose from their teacups while spoons created gentle whirlpools in the hot liquid. "Professor," she said uneasily, "please tell me more about both houses."

He did not like the cold, impersonal title. He would have much preferred her to use his birth name, but he was hesitant to correct her. He said, "Some houses possess a sense of invulnerability. Mt. Ebal in its other locations has existed for 150 years without suffering substantial or any noteworthy damage. It has escaped the wrecking crews on numerous occasions and survived both the War Between the States and the occasional conflicts with the two surrounding Indian nations, the Cherokee and Creek. Why would it not last another 150 years? Have I not saved it from destruction? Does it not owe me a debt of gratitude?"

The Professor paused to sip his tea, then continued, "When I arrived after work one day, with the objective of painting the bedroom walls, I noticed that one of the lower panes of the front entryway transom had been broken. On the porch, in front of the shattered antique glass, was a pool of fresh blood. Upon entering the hallway, I found no object, such as a rock, that could have been used in breaking the glass. Like the broken marble top counter in the kitchen, had someone used their hand in an emotional outburst? The incident only tended to confirm my feeling of the house's invincibility or was this sensation only a figment of my own imagination? Was the house gradually becoming more important than my own family or even me? Like a tumor, Mt. Ebal had imbedded itself deep within my organs. I knew too well that it was slowly consuming me."

As he spoke, he admired her facial features and her curiosity. He dared not stare into her eyes for that would confirm his growing attraction to her. He did not desire to admit to himself that he was still capable of not only being sexually aroused, but of loving another more than the house, the extension of his very soul. "What madness, she is a stranger," he thought.

Robin felt compelled to mention a recent occurrence that had troubled her. "I had a most strange dream in color two nights ago," she said. "Does the name Anna mean anything to you? That was the name of the woman in my dream. The setting was Gatlinburg. It was indeed a strange setting for a dream. As you may know, the town is located at the foot of the Great Smoky Mountains National Park. It is a place where it would be nice to meet and write since the town is a resort area with abundant walks and tall mountains. It also has a cheap carnival atmosphere that lends itself to the creation of characterizations."

Robin looked down at the tabletop as she continued, "In the dream, a person named Anna and you were in a 1930s style lodge; the type that was built during the Great Depression. The walls were stained pine and the floor was soft wood, the type that creaks and gives way to footsteps just like the floor in this house. A lamp sat unevenly on the floor with its shade slightly tilted. The hall was wide and the rooms opened into it from each side. All of the room doors were open."

Robin paused for a moment as she looked at a primitive painting of a woman hanging on the wall nearby. "You and Anna were both naked. Other colleagues and friends entered the room at random, exchanged pleasantries with you both, then left. You responded physically to Anna's nudity, yet did not touch her. You were both engrossed in a conversation I cannot recall. You sat in an old green leather easy chair that wore the patina of age. She was seated in a relaxed fashion at the edge of the bed, and then I awoke. I know it does not mean anything, but the dream was so real. I felt like I was there. Like in a film, I was an observer that could only look upon a scene."

The Professor hid his concern. "No, I don't know a person named Anna. It is, however, a common name."

She had not been attracted to him at the conference. In fact, the Professor was the kind of man that others avoided because they sensed his need to be alone. She had hesitantly been seated next to him. Deep valleys created by sun exposure outlined his lips; his eyes yielded an aged expression.

Unlike the young men of Spanish descent that she had met in Baja, he was freckled as the fall leaves that rest hesitantly upon the nearby forest floor. His emotionless expression yielded little relief to the indecision she had felt upon first looking at him. Like the Phantom of the Opera, the mask he wore was his writing. His words, gathered to form expressions, had attracted her. Haunting words, that when woven as a tapestry of Mt. Ebal's history, both intrigued and disturbed her.

Robin looked towards the Professor. "In an e-mail as well as in our conversation on our way to Mt. Ebal from Atlanta, you mentioned you had two homes destroyed, one by fire and one by a tornado. Tell me more about what happened to the Texas house? I am sure that it too has a story."

The Professor replied, "Yes, it does. I have tried within my thoughts to establish the relationship beyond that which we have already discussed. Oddly, one object ties the two houses together: a broken mirror.

"As my father and I drove down a street in Galveston, Texas in the 1950s, he noticed a wrecking crew at work on a great mansion that stood on the corner of a street near the University of Texas Medical School. The home had been built prior to the 1900 Galveston hurricane when the island was the economic and trade center of Texas. Great summer homes for the wealthy Victorians appeared throughout the community. Their foundations were only a few feet above sea level.

"The vacant mansion, near the end of its life, had once housed a medical fraternity but now it stood in the way of more parking space or perhaps an addition to the campus. All that remained as I viewed the house were the main parlor and a staircase that led into the sky no longer surrounded by walls. At the base of the staircase was a small door that opened under the stairwell. Columns supporting only the coastal clouds still stood erect in the open hall whose walls had been removed by careless, yet determined, force."

"The parlor's mantelpiece and the ornate mirror resting upon it had not yet been completely destroyed even though the inevitable demolition of the house was evident. The mirror was beveled and placed within a large frame supported by two exotic wood columns. A portion of the mirror's surface was missing from a blow and a large crack ran diagonally across the left portion of glass. Its thickness had prevented the glass from shattering completely. As a child, I remember looking up at it and noticing a faint image within the glass. The image appeared to be that of a woman's face. Since my father did not mention it, I don't think he ever saw it.

"A child's imagination can create shapes in clouds that do not exist. You say to a fiend 'look,' but then it is gone. Later when I moved the mirror to Mt. Ebal, I did not see the face. I must have just imagined it as a child. Funny, how I just thought of that face from so long ago. I still wonder, however, what force had struck the mirror and why? Perhaps it was vandals.

"The contractor responsible for the destruction and removal of the house sold my father all remaining artifacts for fifteen dollars and was happy to have them hauled off. As I left, the bulldozer collapsed the staircase and the few remaining walls. My father's purchases remained on the street corner in disarray waiting for us to return later with a trailer.

"With the close of the school year, the doors and mantelpiece were transported to our cotton farm and consequently installed within our Victorian farmhouse. The twelve-foot doors were reduced to eleven to accommodate the farmhouse's twelve-foot ceiling. The mirror was placed above the primitive farmhouse mantel that was in the living room."

"Before the farmhouse fire, I moved the mantelpiece to Mt. Ebal. There I covered the broken portion with artificial ivy. It once more became the centerpiece of a room and was noted by visitors for its unmatched reflection and ornate frame.

"This small almost trivial fact did link the two houses in a physical and material way in that the mirror had been attached above the mantels in the two houses and both were destroyed."

The Professor's eyes blinked as lightning struck nearby followed by a loud clap. He continued, "The parallel, at least to me, was striking. The mirror was on the verge of being destroyed by the wrecking crew in Galveston, the fire in the farmhouse and was finally crushed under the weight of the chimney at Mt. Ebal. Nothing remains of the once grand Galveston mansion except a small fragment of one of the mirror's supporting columns. It sits now in the basement of a rental house that I own."

The Professor asked Robin a question, "Isn't there a West Indies belief that if you keep something from the spirit world, the dead never leave you? Some have used mirrors in an attempt to contact the departed. A local author, who is also an M.D, has written several books about contacting the dead through the use of mirrors. After the tornado, he sent me a copy of his book on near-death experiences."

"Why did he send you a copy of his book?" questioned Robin.

The Professor hesitated, then replied, "I thought I might have had a near-death experience, so I called him and described what happened to me when the twister struck the house."

She looked uncomfortably at him. "You really know how to set the stage for a good night's sleep."

Banks of thunderheads were suspended above and around them providing intermittent flashes of light followed by the thunder's crushing sound and distant echo. Their conversation continued as rain fell.

The Professor smiled at her. "It is strange how dreams can affect what we feel. A week ago I dreamed of a young woman in a white dress sitting on my side porch. There were wildflowers on a table before her. I can still clearly see her face. She was crying loudly. When I asked her what was wrong, she only said, 'My name is Annie.' Odd that you mentioned Anna earlier. I had forgotten what the name was in my dream until now." He paused. "When I awoke, I was covered in sweat. The strangest thing was to occur a week later.

"I was walking up the stairs of Bibb Graves, our administrative building. Another person was descending, her back lit by the large windows. She was wearing clothing very out of tune with today's student fashions: a full-length skirt and a faded flowery blouse. Her skin, hair, eyes and expression were those of a person without emotion. A chill ran through me, and I did not look back as I continued to ascend the staircase. I am certain it was the same person in my dream."

Robin commented, "I think there is a connection between the past and future and that bridge is our dreams. How else can you explain seeing people that seem so familiar to you when the two of you have never met?" She added in an apologetic manner, "I know I am not explaining myself very well, perhaps I can tomorrow when I feel more refreshed."

The Professor assumed she was ready to retire for the evening, but suddenly Robin asked once again to know more about Mt. Ebal.

"There is so much additional history to tell. Since we are so tired, please forgive me if I repeat myself. As I mentioned earlier, a house approaching two hundred years old experiences all the common and uncommon events of life. Because it predated the concept of the modern hospital or clinic, births occurred within the house. At that time in history, the cemeteries were filled with infants whose mothers died at childbirth when happiness should have been the greatest emotion, but instead the hour often yielded uncontrollable grief."

"The dead were placed in the large halls of the homes and watched over by those who loved them. The purpose of the vigil was not only to honor the dead, but also to protect them from rats and other animals that frequented Alabama's first dwellings. Many of the earliest Alabama homes had a dogtrot that opened to nature at both ends of the log houses.

"As I previously mentioned, the home served not only as a hospital but also as a funeral home. The two front entryway doors of the large hall soon became known as funeral doors. They were large enough to allow a coffin to be carried through the portal on its way for burial. It was later those two doors I pressed against in an attempt to close them while the tornado ripped like a saw through the house. It appeared that I too was to pass through those portals to Mt. Ebal cemetery."

"During my first visit to the house with the realtor, she mentioned that a Ms. Anna Whiten had died while walking from a backroom into the bedroom. Even though she was in her forties, she died of an apparent heart attack. Ms. Whiten had been a well-respected artist and faculty member. The place on the floor where she died was later crushed by the falling chimney."

He glanced at Robin for a moment. He wondered if he had been correct in mentioning the house and suggesting her visit. The plan to have four days of intensive creative writing seemed harmless enough. She, he had hoped, would be able to contribute a feminine perspective while he concentrated on the events surrounding the house. Together, they would collaborate, adding to the storyline, including stream of consciousness sequences.

Was such a plan delusional? He paused for a moment, he had forgotten Ms. Whiten's first name until that moment. He looked again at Robin. For a brief instant, he looked at her as a man would and not as a fellow collaborator. He felt her presence; needed her presence in his analytical world of emotionless data.

There was no doubt that the Professor felt attracted to her, but he feared that such attraction would diminish the professional tasks to be undertaken by their meeting. He must remain objective for the data to be valid.

He had reached out to her without touching. Could such a relationship last? His perfectly ordered life had shown its greatest flaw. The scholar's actions demonstrated urges repressed by his degrees and position. Was she any more real than Anna or had he also created her presence?

The Professor continued his discussion, "My dreams have always been in color. They are usually full of physical action or tasks that need to be completed. Unlike in a typical night, the sleep before the storm did not produce any dreams for me. It was exactly the opposite for the person I loved.

"As we sat in the parlor in the early morning hours of Palm Sunday, drinking coffee, we began to talk. My son had not yet stirred. My wife mentioned being awakened from a deep sleep by a very disturbing dream. The main character in her dream was her deceased mother. It was very unusual because she had never dreamed of her since her untimely death fourteen years earlier. The dream further disturbed her because her mother asked one very pointed question, 'Why do you look so sad?' At that point, she woke up. She turned towards me and asked, 'I wonder what that meant?' In a few hours, the answer would be revealed in the screams of fear and wind."

Fire-cast shadows moved across the walls. The Professor continued, "We spent the evening watching rented videos. There was nothing out of the ordinary about the movies. My younger son did not like to watch anything frightening but preferred titles such as *Treasure Island* or *Raiders of the Lost Ark*. My wife usually read during the videos. I loved being with my son and the movies provided an avenue of discussion and reflected our mutual love for literature, film and art.

"I wanted the next day to be perfect, free from fatigue. I excused myself and went to bed early having been at work that day. The evening was comfortable and did not require the use of covers. I lay in bed, thinking about what I would like to do the following day. I was hoping to plant pecan trees and crape myrtles. The evening seemed in harmony and was filled with the pleasures of companionship and love.

"My eyes remained open as I studied the ceiling above me. Suddenly I was filled with terror. My body felt frozen as though encased in solid ice. The cold penetrated my body and at first I was unable to move. As quickly as it came, the extreme cold vanished and I was able to get to my feet. I then hurried back to my family – my wife was still reading and my son was watching another movie. I did not share the incident with my wife until the following day for fear of disturbing the relaxed mood of the evening.

"This state of being frozen has only occurred once in my life. I am unable to explain the sensation of cold that must be what death is like at the moment of the soul's departure. Had death embraced me that evening or was it an unseen presence seeking the warmth denied to it by time?"

- 13 -
A Plea

The Professor continued, "My youngest son begged to go to church on Palm Sunday, but I told him it was such a beautiful day that it would be fun for us to stay home. After all, we planned to attend the evening church services. Inwardly, I had no intention of leaving my dream even for my faith. He continued to beg which was odd, considering that attending church was not something any ten-year-old had ever looked forward to, but accepted it as a responsibility to be overseen by their parents. I needed a day to convince both myself and my family that I made the right decision in moving to Mt. Ebal. Was it boredom, isolation, faith or fear that drove my son's pleas? A premonition unheard by me."

For a moment, as he and Robin talked, the lights flickered. The Professor was quick to assure Robin that it was the result of nearby lightning strikes upon the mountain peaks. The Professor then added, "Unlike my home in Texas, we seldom have power losses at Mt. Ebal. We did experience, however, on numerous occasions, lights that would go off in the bedroom. We would be in the parlor and after an hour or two of reading, we would return to the darkened bedroom. We would ask each other if the other one had turned the lamp off. The problem was not in the circuitry or in the bedroom lamp for it had been physically turned off. We would laugh and accuse the other of being forgetful. How else could it be cut off? It must have been our forgetfulness. To answer otherwise would have endangered my quest."

Though his body fought against the will to sleep, the Professor felt the urge to continue. He looked into her expectant eyes, then glanced away to the fire that he had just restarted. "Let me tell you about what happened to my mother. Like I said, she was very excited about moving to Mt. Ebal. My father had suffered a stroke while having hip surgery and was unable to move. His mind remained sharp in spite of his paralyzed condition. After their arrival, I noticed Mother was changing. Her optimism dwindled and dread took its place. One day, while visiting me at work, she said she could hear a person calling her. When I asked whose voice it was, she stated that it was mine.

"I remember the farmhouse and the summer night conversations of people who did not exist except to amuse our parlor guest. Her statement now was all too eerily familiar. I dismissed it as only the sound of the wind, a chimney's echo, as interpreted by her feelings of isolation intensified by moving away from the Texas farm, her friends, family and the despondency related to Father's worsening condition.

"She insisted, however, that the voice was mine, and that I was calling to her just as I used too when I was a child on the farm. It was my practice to always shout, 'It's me, Mom!' before entering the kitchen door in order not to frighten her.

"No matter what explanation I gave her, she was persistent in her belief that the voice was real. Her attitude towards the house was rapidly changing as my own would soon be."

Robin shifted her position as the Professor continued, "As Mother's depression and Father's physical condition worsened, she became more insistent that I move them from the house. She repeatedly told me that something bad was going to happen to the house and to those within it. Finally in November 1993, she said that she did not care where I moved them as long as it was away from Mt. Ebal and the hill upon which it stood. She did not care if it were to a park or a prison; she and my father would not stay at Mt. Ebal.

"I was very sad that she no longer loved what to me was truly a work of wooden art, seasoned by time and history. The antique glass windows, the patina of colors upon the heart of pine flooring and the smell of leather-bound books fermented by time were as intoxicating to me as the perfumed women that I had earlier known as a sailor.

"With regret, I quickly found them a home in Anniston, Alabama. Mother did not mention the house again nor would she explain her premonition. She felt safe in the new house with its vaulted ceiling, vinyl siding and carpeting. I now, of course, realize that her fears saved their lives and my own doubt was to cast both myself and my family into peril."

☙

The Professor, after offering more tea to Robin, explained, "The sun shone hot in the midsummer Alabama afternoon. We sat on the porch hoping to catch a breath of air, but it was denied us. The hilltop was void of motion and only the insects reminded us that life continued and we had not become painted characters in an artist's canvas. My wife sat in the large porch swing while I lounged in a nearby chair across her. Shadows played upon the stage.

"As we talked, a hanging pot planted with various flowers began to rotate. It would turn clockwise and stop, only to reverse its rotation. I wondered where the current of wind was coming from since there was not any breeze upon my skin. As I continued to talk to my wife and watch the hanging basket, I noticed the flowers parting down the middle. One portion bent to the left and the other half bent to the right as though hands were tending or searching through the small, hanging garden.

"There before me, like a vision in a dream, appeared the faint silhouettes of three people who appeared like vapors in a summer's mirage. I do not know if what I saw was real or not. Perhaps I had sat too long and the blood had pooled to my legs or the vision was caused by my forgetting to take my blood pressure medicine, which unfortunately happens too often.

"I shouted for my wife to look. She too noticed the movement of the hanging garden. When we approached the basket, the flowers resumed their vertical stance and the hanging plant no longer rotated.

We discussed the odd incident and soon withdrew to the recently air-conditioned interior of the house.

"I did not mention the silhouettes that I had seen. I am now convinced that they must have been shadows created by clouds or vapors rising from the porch floor. After all, I had watered the plants earlier that morning.

"For the last two centuries, a tornado has struck the exact same position on Mt. Ebal. When I purchased the land, I was curious about the odd depressions found throughout the property. A resident of the area told me they were Indian graves. The realtor, however, said they were pits dug by prospectors who were testing for iron ore deposits. Later a person in his 70s, having lived near the mountain all of his life, told me they were the result of tree roots that had been pulled right off the ground, like nothing more than planted corn, in the 1800s by a tornado that destroyed the mountain community. A story that had been told to him by his grandfather.

"After the 1994 tornado, I was to see how the pits were formed. Entire root systems were lifted from the earth creating holes as deep as eight feet. It is obvious that the storm had followed the exact path. I have juxtaposed a troubled house with a violent mountain. Is it any wonder that events with no scientific explanation were occurring?"

He continued, his face occasionally key-lit by lightning, with the happenings of the two parallel houses, "If you sat quietly near the fireplace on a warm summer night at the Texas farmhouse, you could hear what sounded like a room full of people talking in casual conversation. It was similar to the indistinguishable chatter of a New Orleans' restaurant. Some evenings, my parents would invite company to listen to the sound. In that the farmhouse was more than a mile from the nearest neighbor, such chatter was even more unusual. Occasionally, a distinct word could be heard or even the sound of a solitary piano playing Chopin.

"The unusual sounds soon took the character of a parlor game as guests would add their interpretations as to what was being heard. The farmhouse is now a burned out ruin. Perhaps, the great room is silent."

Robin looked at him having noticed that his expression had changed. Her blue eyes making contact with his, she said, "There must have been more events that occurred. Tell me about them and, by the way, I could use another cup of tea."

"Are you sure you want to hear more? You must be tired." His words sounded from the kitchen. "Remember that the tea is very hot."

"Thank you, please continue. This is why I journeyed to Mt. Elba after returning from Hawaii, where I was supposed to meet my son. I did not want to go directly to a house without him, even though I really need to be at work. I am not strong enough to be alone at this moment," she said with convincing sincerity. Her blue eyes framed by a smile that quickly dimmed. "My son has volunteered for military service. I keep thinking of the poem I memorized years before by W. B. Yeats – it seems very appropriate to me now." She spoke softly while looking away towards the Southern storm thumping upon the antique glass.

I know that I shall meet my fate
Somewhere among the clouds above;
Those that I fight I do not hate,
Those that I guard I do not love;
My county is Kiltartan Cross,
My countrymen Kiltartan's poor,
No likely end could bring them loss
Or leave them happier than before.
Nor law, nor duty bade me fight,
Nor public man, nor cheering crowds,
A lonely impulse of delight
Drove to this tumult in the clouds;
I balanced all, brought all to mind,
The years to come seemed waste of breath,
A waste of breath the years behind
In balance with this life, this death.

For a moment, the Professor felt the human sentiment of profound grief. The words of Yeats pierced his memory and filled him with emotions. His hand trembled briefly, then he regained his composure, his eyes moistened by the memory of his Vietnam unit's final roll call long since repressed.

❧

"It is interesting to note," continued the Professor, *"that when I rebuilt the house, I noticed that the hall walls were of a later period of construction.* Mill-sized timber had been used. In addition, the tongue-in-groove lumber was attached to studs in which round-headed nails had been used. One way to date a house is to determine the nail type that had been used in the construction.

"A house is like a human body, it bears its scars both inside and out."

The Professor attempted to hide his yawn, but he felt too emotional to cease in his description. "The method used in constructing the hall walls was in strong contrast to the rest of the house where the supporting timbers had been pegged. It dawned on me that the house must have suffered some type of severe damage prior to being been moved from the countryside to the village of Ladigaville." He looked at Robin who seemed to be still interested. "Unfortunately, the room where the columned porch had formerly been was totally destroyed by the tornado. The result was that I could not study the original construction nor date it as a reference. The more I thought about it, the more the house seems like an illusion, an image created by mirrors. The proportions were only correct as determined by your position. If you altered your perspective, the dimensions of the house would change as well."

❧

The Professor, his voice weakening, said, "The hill upon which the house rested had been the site of several former homes. Towards the back of the property, I located plants from a different time period. Some refer to them now as antique, which I assume means they no longer have any commercial value. You know, the hues of the roses are not as red.

These types of plants no longer find favor with gardeners. They are indicative of a time period before hybridization and are not as ornamental as plants sold in today's highly competitive marketplace. I imagine they were hardier in that they flourished in a time period before the widespread use of commercial insecticides."

The Professor looked at Robin and then towards the unattended fire. "I am now faced with confronting a house that I both love and fear. If I did not know its troubled past, I would have found a few days alone in the country refreshing – lazily sitting on the porch reading, drinking coffee and being immersed in a world of sights, sounds, and feelings. Each of my five senses finely attuned to the environment. Body bare to the wind's touch, feet upon cool floors. Breaths of blooming mountain flowers deeply inhaled.

"It is not the sun that I dread but the shadows, I know inwardly that whatever form it may take, the tornado will return to Mt. Ebal as it has for the past two centuries and perhaps centuries before that. I cannot seem to escape my attraction to the house or the approaching winds of another storm."

Robin replied, "What was it like being in the funnel of a tornado? I cannot imagine how terrifying it must have been."

The Professor looked away before replying. "I avoided your earlier question about why I thought I had a near-death experience. Some memories are very difficult to face. So forgive me for my earlier hesitation.

"As I previously said, we were playing a board game called LIFE. The game's play money was blown off the card table and was floating on rising air currents. I then called to my wife who was seated in the adjoining bedroom to help my son and me to pick up the money. She put down her copy of *Southern Living* reluctantly and entered the hallway to collect the currency alongside us. Suddenly, the wind grew so intense it blew the front doors open."

The Professor picked up the now cool cup of tea and continued, "Little did we realize that the tornado was moving from the southwest while the double doors faced the northeast. We, therefore, did not see the approaching funnel cloud. Had we seen it in sufficient time, we would have raced to the iron caboose that would prove to be an excellent storm shelter. As we closed the two doors, the wind continued to bluster with an occasional burst of hail hitting the front porch. Then the sun would appear again only to be followed by the sound of hail hitting the wood-shingled roof. The cycles were repeated in an ever shortening sequence of events.

"The doors flew open again even though we had locked them by then. As I used my right shoulder to push the door against the wind, I could see a dark elliptical shape moving across the grass. My wife screamed, 'Tornado!' and released her pressure against the other door. I had never seen a tornado before except as a waterspout over Chesapeake Bay while in the Navy and over Galveston Bay when I lived on the island as a child. My wife, however, had been in the Dallas tornado in the 1950s and recognized the sound and the pattern of spiraling debris. Having freed her grip from the door, she immediately fled into the parlor accompanied by my son. The force of the wind pushed me back until it was impossible to stand upright. One cannot deter an F4 tornado from entering the front door.

"I found myself falling to the entryway floor. Immediately all sounds stopped and all around me was a light of brilliant gold color. In movies, showing a spotlight or backlight upon a person often depicts this. It is not possible to demonstrate this in film for it requires a total immersion in light."

Robin could see small drops of sweat on his forehead as he spoke.

"There was no source to the light, but I was floating upon currents of light totally free of any feelings except for uttermost contentment. There was no sensation of pain nor was there any fear. Like a gauge in the cockpit of an airplane, I saw a hand on edge that was symbolically moving between life and death. It appeared to be rendering a judgment whether I was to live or die. I knew that if it moved left, death was inevitable. Time was suddenly suspended in a deliberation of life and death.

"Suddenly I was on the floor and all was black. Around me were floating particles of debris. It dawned on me that neither my wife nor my son was with me. I immediately rose and ran towards the parlor where they had fled. Only later did I realize that I had been cut about the legs and that the golden light, in all probability, was sunlight passing through the vortex of the funnel cloud.

"Judging from the boundaries of my property, the F4 funnel had past directly through the entryway. On both sides of the house, my fifteen acres had been evenly clear-cut of all the large and small trees with only a few bent saplings remaining. I had taken great pride in my forest and allowed no one to cut any of the trees even as they encroached upon the house.

"When I returned several weeks later to look at Mt. Ebal, it occurred to me that I was alive only because it was so solidly built. Heavy timbers had braced the hand-hewn frames again the wind. Large square nails had held much of the wide heart of the pine flooring and many of the walls in place.

"The caboose in my backyard with its wheels set upon the rails had been lifted off the track and set down beside it. Previously I had an iron stop welded to one rail to keep vandals from moving it with their automobile. Having jumped the guard, it was blocked only by an earthen embankment and a large tree from traveling down the mountain and perhaps killing others in its potential journey to the Mt. Ebal Baptist Church below.

"The end cap of one of the new chimneys crashed through the floor at my feet. There were no front walls to the entryway remaining nor was there a ceiling above me. There was no furniture left in the hall – everything had been swept out the front door or through the open ceiling. In the adjoining bedroom where my wife had previously been seated, one of the two end chimneys had also fallen through the floor to the ground. All of the furniture was missing from the front room or now lay beneath the bricks. No ceiling or outer walls remained in the bedroom area.

"The doors that I had pressed against in my attempt to keep out the wind were more than 150 feet from the house. I knew I should be dead along with the other twenty or thirty people killed by the Palm Sunday tornado. In a sense I did die, for all of my dreams ended at that moment."

A bolt of lightning hit nearby, causing the power in the house to fluctuate.

"Now I realized that I must die twice. It would have been so easy to die in the funnel – no fear, no pain, silence and an extreme feeling of contentment I had never experienced before or since. In a sense, I feel that I am both living and dead. A man cheated of ultimate grace."

"As a side item of interest," continued the Professor, "I also realized that I was one of the few people to have been in the eye of a hurricane on a ship and in the vortex of a tornado on land and have lived through both experiences. As events turned out, there was no great purpose in my living; no grand plan involved.

"My insurance agent and a prospective builder both told me that there was nothing left of the house to build upon. The only cost-effective option was to tear down the remaining portion of the structure or burn it as it stood. When a friend found out about the destruction of the house, he offered to remove the debris in exchange for what was left of the flooring since heartwood pine flooring is truly beautiful and valuable. Being too depressed to either accept or reject his offer, I did not return his phone calls nor reply to his frequent e-mails.

"I had an early Macintosh 512K computer at home with a program called MacPaint that was loaded using a disk. While using the program, I began to draw various squares and rectangles. Having previously studied Greek Revival architecture, I began to draw shapes that represented a cottage. Then it dawned on me, if a person in 1850 had this technology available to him, what architectural renderings might he have made? Using the computer-generated images, I attempted to recreate the original structure using as much of the salvaged wood as possible. The end result was my plan to rebuild Mt. Ebal."

He then added, "Unfortunately, I had several professional builders examine the site. One by one, they left saying they were not interested in the job. When a friend mentioned hiring a young man to tin a barn, I contacted the young man. He was very enthusiastic about the project, but admitted that his only experience had been in replacing a metal roof on a barn or, as he called it, "tinning a barn." Even though he hired two additional workers to help him, both of them quit and left him to work on the project alone. Day by day, the work progressed almost as if a miracle were occurring. I would go out one day and there would be no wall to a particular room. The next day it would be in place. The most amazing event occurred when he was able to lift the collapse hall wall by himself and put it in place. Not only was the wall a dead lift, but a portion of it had been buried in the debris field. I still do not know what he did to perform the impossible."

捓

Robin created mental images of the events that he described. "I waited until now to bring up the manuscript that you sent. I wanted us to be able to review it together. There is a contract to be signed. It is a standard form used by many publishers. I tried to get you the best financial deal possible. I have to admit that publishing a story about a house, even a truly haunted one, is not an easy sell."

She looked very serious as she spoke. "I know you denied having sent the manuscript to me. It was, however, mailed from the post office in Ladigaville, Alabama just little over a month ago. The moment I read it, I knew it had value. My trying to get an appointment with a publisher proved to be the greatest challenge. Fortunately, I knew the publisher from my own literary efforts. After he had an opportunity to review the manuscript, he called me right up.

"I admit I was surprised that you had not sent it as registered mail. The included illustrations appear to be the originals. Something this valuable is usually sent with some degree of assurance that it has been received. It was apparent why you didn't send it as an e-mail attachment. The beautifully colored illustrations that abound throughout the manuscript would certainly have made it a prohibitive file size. Like I said on the phone, you should have mentioned your artistic talent as an illustrator."

The Professor looked at her inquisitively. "Robin, I still don't know what you are talking about. You mentioned illustrations. I can only draw matchstick characters to represent people. I never progressed beyond a third grade level in art."

Robin responded, laughing, "You are kidding me? I assumed that your denial was a trick to get me here or to serve as a literary icebreaker for our first serious discussion related to a contract. You are probably the most modest man I have ever met."

The Professor looked at her intently. "Robin, did you bring the manuscript with you? I would like to see what you received."

Robin hesitated, then replied, "Yes, I did. It is in my luggage. Just a moment and I will get it for you." She rose from the table and walked towards the guest bedroom where she had left her luggage sitting atop the bed. A nearby owl she had heard upon entering the house began calling as she rotated her luggage so that the zipper faced her. As she unzipped her suitcase, a small spot of light slowly moved across the innermost wall. Then all was dark except for the light provided by a distant flash of retreating lightning. As quickly as the electricity had vanished, it reappeared with the glow of the incandescent light.

At first startled, she regained her composure as she heard a car traveling somewhere down the road below the house. "It must have been," she thought, "the neighbor's headlights flashing on the bedroom wall as they left their home." She paused for a moment and became briefly concerned when she remembered that Mt. Ebal was far above the nearest neighbors' driveway. Also, the woods were thick with the new growth of both pine and cedar, preventing the beam of headlights from reaching the house.

Upon returning to the parlor, she placed the large binder-clipped volume before him. He immediately saw why she had been so impressed. The actual title of the book belonged to him: *Lost Graves*. In addition, he noticed that the title had been written with a calligraphy pen. The handwriting style was beautiful and reminiscent of the 19th-century documents he had recently seen on display in a recreated village of the Old South in Montgomery. The paper used was crisp and new. He turned the pages rapidly until he came upon a strikingly beautiful illustration of Mt. Ebal. There, on the mountaintop sat the white house surrounded by large trees and gardens. It was beautifully rendered. The illustration depicted a large horse with a military saddle secured to a hitching post. Wisteria grew abundantly upon the side porch columns. The original illustration appeared to have been done in watercolor since there was an inherent softness in the light. Seated on the porch, though small at a distance, was a woman in a light-colored dress, her hair cast carelessly about her shoulder, drinking what appeared to be tea. Nearby on the porch was a large man in some type of period clothing, looking down at her. It was apparently early spring since the rose bushes, fruit trees and wisteria were beginning to have buds.

The titles and captions of the illustrations were handwritten in a most beautiful printing style. The remaining narrative itself seemed to have been composed using a typewriter or a computer. As he rapidly flipped through the pages, he noted that the text adhered more or less to the outline he had previously sent to her. "Could it be," he thought, "that she took my outline and wrote the narrative herself? After all, it has been several weeks since I sent the outline to her." He knew from having seen her website that she was an illustrator of great talent. "Yes, that must be it. She is playing a game with me."

"Robin," he said loudly, "you are teasing me! I am very flattered that you liked my outline enough to write the narrative for the book. What amazes me is that you did it in such a short period of time. You obviously took some of the pictures of the house and the tornado from the website posted by the news bureau at my university and used them as the base for some of your illustrations. You are indeed a very clever and truly gifted writer and illustrator."

Robin looked at him, taken back by his accusation and the tone of his voice. She knew she had not written the manuscript, but sensed that he seemed genuinely startled when he saw the illustrations. She realized also that the matter was not settled and that they would need to discuss the manuscript further at a later time.

- 14 -
A NIGHT ALONE

Robin did not reply to his accusatory statement regarding the authorship of the manuscript. She could not control the yawn that she visually expressed. The day had been very long and so had been the drive to Mt. Ebal from the train station in Atlanta.

The Professor immediately caught the hint. "Robin, you must be exhausted. We can talk about the manuscript tomorrow. Let me show you the bath." As they walked towards the bathroom, he pointed to the guest bedroom where she had left her luggage. "I hope that you will find the bed very comfortable. I bought a feather mattress from an older lady who said it was made by her grandmother. Since this is a guestroom and I have not entertained since the rebuilding of the house, no one has slept upon it."

At the end of the hallway was the bath. Obviously it had been a porch at one time. The outside wall consisted of tall glass windows that reached from floor to ceiling. Near the center of the room was an antique iron tub with a slight degree of rust on the edges and areas exposed by several small cracks in the porcelain. The bathroom lights reflected an image of the space upon the glass windowpanes. Occasionally, lightning could be seen followed by thunder that echoed from the mountains and hollows of the Appalachians.

At the very end of the bathroom was a full-length mirror while other large mirrors of various sizes and degrees of refinements graced the other walls. The full-length mirror was placed within a gilded frame that bore an ornate crest upon the top portion. It was also apparent that any image seen within it would be distorted, a reflection of its age.

The Professor noted her staring at the mirror. "Oh, do you find it interesting? Finding a mirror of that size and age was difficult. It came from an old Louisiana plantation home, now destroyed, known as Woodlawn. At least the person who sold it to me claimed that it did. You can never tell the true origin of antiques. In addition, one can only guess at their age. It is so easy now to make anything new look aged." He continued, "I am fascinated by old homes and the stories that they reveal. What attracted me to Mt. Ebal was not only its past but also the feeling that a story was still formulating within its walls. A feeling that this house was not a museum that reflected only the past, but a living object that could alter the lives of those who owned or dwelt within." As he spoke, his own exhaustion became apparent to him. Perhaps his prolonged excitement contributed to his fatigue.

She followed him back down the hall, stopping at the entrance of the guest bedroom. He turned around and bid her a good night. She could hear his fading footsteps on the worn pine floor as he walked towards his bedroom.

Robin noticed that he had placed her larger luggage near a four-poster bed. What struck her was that the bed appeared to be handmade from wood that apparently had been collected from a wreck site. The boards did not fit correctly and some were split. Each piece bore weathered and uneven paint. Some boards had multiple layers of paint on them that revealed different colors. The thickness of the wood indicated that it had been hand-milled.

Then it occurred to her that the bed, in all probability, had been constructed from the debris left by the tornado that destroyed so much of the house. In the muted light of the room, the bed appeared like an intruder. It did not belong to her expectation of refined antiques from the antebellum South. Perhaps the original bed had been destroyed in the funnel cloud.

Robin undressed before a large mirror in the room. The bathrobe felt warm on her chilled body. As she looked at her features, she noticed that the color of her hair was darker than she remembered it. Her image also appeared distorted as she peered into the large looking glass. It was as though she had become a voyeur, looking upon another's body.

Robin then walked softly to the bathroom. Steam rose from the bathtub as it filled with hot water. The rising heat mixing with the night air created condensation upon the windowpanes. Robin felt somewhat uneasy as she looked at her naked reflection on the window glass that bore no shutters. In that the house was very remote, it only bothered her for a moment. The touch of warm water removed her brief apprehension.

As Robin relaxed for the first time since leaving her home in upstate New York, she thought she heard a conversation coming from the parlor. It sounded like two men and a woman talking. Even though she lay very still in the tub, she could not make out what was being said. At times there was silence only to be punctuated by the *drip-drip* of water from the faucet.

"That's not possible," Robin thought. "Surely the Professor cannot be having newly arrived company now." The late hour and the storm made that too apparent. "Maybe his television set is emitting more than static? Yes, that is it, the storm must have improved the reception." Still she remained uneasy. The sounds of people talking were just too real to dismiss as emanating from a television set. Then the conversations ceased and the house was silent again except for the hall clock and the drip of water. Occasionally, a popping sound from the fireplace could be heard.

The steam from the bath coated the windows and the mirrors with moisture. As she bathed, the uneasy feeling began to reemerge as though someone was staring at her. As she poured hot water from her cupped hands onto her face, she looked towards the gilded mirror. Beneath the condensation was the image of her body in the tub but the face was not her own. The face appeared to be featureless. She squinted thinking that the soapy water had gotten into her eyes, momentarily blurring her vision. Her heart beat with extreme intensity as she raised herself from the bath, her hands slipping on the porcelain.

Looking once more towards the mirror, she found her own image greeting her. "What is happening here?" she thought. "Did I drink something hallucinogenic?"

Robin dried herself with the soft, warm white bath towel. Upon entering the house, she had noticed a front room just off the hall, its solid oak door closed. She wondered why the Professor had not opened it since the rest of the house appeared to be so open. Perhaps it was his study; a place of privacy, an academician's chapel.

She donned her cashmere robe and warm slippers. Her curiosity had earlier been piqued by what she thought was a conversation coming from that area of the house. "I don't think he would object if I opened the door and peeked in. What would it hurt?" she thought. She reasoned that the Professor must sleep in the bedroom far back – a portion of the house now silent.

She walked quietly upon the wide-planked pine flooring. The boards squeaked softly beneath her weight as she turned the doorknob. It opened without protest. There, before her on the wall, was a mirror that reflected television snow and seated before the set was a woman. She was dressed in 19th-century clothing. Robin's first inclination was to apologize for the intrusion, but then she looked again. The woman was wearing a Mardi Gras mask – bluish green in color with small rubies encircling it. A mask the type of which she had never seen before even on her trip to Venice. Neither the eyes nor the body of the woman moved as Robin stared at her.

"It must be a mannequin! What type of perversion is this?" she said softly to herself. "I will confront the Professor about this in the morning. I know there must be a good explanation. He does not seem the type to purchase a sex toy. It must be an antique that he obtained, yet why is the black-and-white TV set on? Since the shutters are not completely closed, I should have noticed the set being on when we walked up the porch steps. I don't remember any light coming from that area when we arrived."

After additional thought, Robin said to herself, "No, I will wait for him to bring the subject up."

Having gotten into bed, she noted the immediate comfort of the bed. The feather mattress quickly adjusted to the shape of her body and would, after frequent use, result in a permanent pattern of a person's body. The more she considered it, the more it occurred to her that the shape of a body already existed in the bed. It was as though her body had been superimposed upon that of another. The impression in the mattress felt much larger.

"I thought the Professor said that no one had slept upon this bed since it arrived at the house," she recalled. "I would like to ask him about it, but I am too tired, and besides, he is already asleep. It probably retains the shape of someone in the distant past who once slept upon it."

She lay awake thinking about the events of such a long and somewhat troubling day. The feeling of unease persisted as she lay upon the soft bed. An uneasiness compounded by the image within her mind of the mannequin.

"The Professor is a very nice person, yet he appears to be very lonely," she said out loud in the silence. She continued to ponder why she had come to Mt. Ebal. She loved large cities and never intended to visit the Deep South. What was the purpose of collaboration if the story had already been written? Was this a trick to get her to visit Mt. Ebal or, perhaps, a rationalization within his own mind?

The most troubling question for Robin, however, was why the Professor would not admit he wrote and illustrated the manuscript. If he was inviting her to collaborate, why did he send her a completed manuscript ahead of time? Perhaps he judged his work to be substandard or perhaps incomplete. "Could I have been invited for a more sinister reason, perhaps to become a character in his unfinished book?" The thought bothered Robin. Her body tensed in reaction.

Fear was an emotion unknown to Robin. She had traveled alone throughout Europe as a young woman, sleeping along paths that traversed Switzerland on her way to Lake Como. She remembered the flirtatious Italian men. "All action from the neck up," she thought as she laughed to herself.

Lacking an organized faith, she did not allow the concept of death to trouble her. Robin had often commented to friends, "We just die, that is it. *La mort est la fin.*"

She felt self-assured almost to a fault. Yet now, she was beginning to allow fear to enter her body. "Ridiculous, ridiculous," she said out loud in the quiet room.

Even though the house was silent, she began to hear the faint sound of a woman crying. The sound seemed to be coming from the adjacent porch. At first, she assumed that it originated from some animal in the nearby woods or perhaps from the television set in the front room.

She remembered walking alone along a trail just outside Gatlinburg. It was summer and the cool mountain air felt crisp. She had heard what she thought to be a woman crying in the woods. Instantly a large doe crossed the trail just in front of her at full gallop, pursued by an unseen animal. In the woods there followed the piercing scream of a woman. Suddenly an adult mountain lion ran in front of her in pursuit of the deer, its tail outstretched and ears pulled back. From head to tail, the animal appeared to be seven feet as measured by the width of the trail that it leaped across.

The two animals penetrated deeper into the woods until the lion's screams were no longer heard. Robin had never known that a puma could sound exactly like a woman crying and screaming. Perhaps there were panthers in the woods surrounding Mt. Ebal.

She quickly arose and locked the double porch doors. Once the outside chamber doors were locked, the room fell silent. Robin then also locked her bedroom door by using a large wooden latch. As she walked toward the bed, the wooden floor felt very cool to her feet.

The air within the room seemed to chill as the night wind blew against the antique windowpanes. Robin tossed upon the feather bed. At first she could not sleep. Despite her efforts to remain awake, at last her eyes closed. Then like warm surf passing over the sands of a tropical atoll, she fell asleep, secure under the quilts that covered her body on the feather bed.

Suddenly, she was walking upon a cold floor. Her nightgown rippled in a strong breeze that reached for her legs, a breeze coming from the murder hole beneath her feet. In her hand was a candle that knelt before the strong wind.

Robin walked slowly down a long corridor on roughhewn boards that talked to the castle walls in their moans and creaks. Her steps led her to a room at the end of a hall where flickering candlelight fled from a partially opened door.

As she pushed the chamber door open, she saw the Professor pressing his hips against the mannequin's. Both of their entwined bodies were silhouettes created by the castle's large stone fireplace. Upon the mantelpiece were three stone gargoyles. Robin immediately recognized the stonework as being the same as in Ballindooley Castle. A tower castle located in County Galway that had belonged to her family in the 16th-century. She had visited the castle just before the death of her grandmother, Lady Mary DeBurton, who told her many secrets about the occupants of the castle. The grandmother's stories of betrayal and murder had fascinated the teenage girl.

Slowly both the Professor and Anna turned their wooden faces towards Robin. Their eyes were without expression, like features painted on a canvas. Behind the two lovers was a man standing in the shadows. His hand held a medieval axe. Robin recognized instinctively that it was the betrayed husband of Anna, an incident told through the generations of her family.

Robin immediately awoke from the dream. Smoke from the fireplace was seeping beneath her door, yet the house was now quiet. The flames within the hearth burned silently.

Robin arose from her bed and opened the doors that fronted onto the porch. There standing in the moonlight was a large man whose form was revealed in the moonlight. Robin immediately slammed the door and screamed in terror.

From down the hall, she could hear the Professor running towards her parlor. He flung open her now unlocked chamber door. "What is it? What is it?" he shouted.

"Professor, I smelled smoke coming from under my door. I opened the door to the veranda to vent the odor. There was a man standing just off the porch. A large man revealed in the moonlight."

"Robin, please don't worry. I am sure it was just Larry. He is a special person that I occasionally ask to work in the garden. Larry often walks about the estate at my request. I must admit that I have never known him to walk about the grounds at night. I will talk to him tomorrow about it. Some people have been stealing the vegetables, so I've asked him to occasionally check on the garden."

"Professor, why didn't he say anything to me?"

"Don't worry. As I mentioned before, he has some challenges that the rest of us do not have. He really is a kind person. I am just sorry that I didn't tell you about him before. Now go to bed. We have a lot to talk about tomorrow. Besides, I am just down the hall from you."

Robin locked her doors and stared at the wooden ceiling, awaiting the first light of the dawn. Yet dreams returned as they often did.

Soon Robin felt very drowsy. Then whether awake or asleep she could not recall, through the window that opened to the porch, she could see the moon. It appeared full and red in color, its reflective light masked briefly by rapidly moving clouds.

Suddenly it was bright sun. On the columned porch, two young lovers were talking. Both were dressed in clothing from a much earlier time period. The man wore a coat lined with fine brass buttons while the woman's dress was full length. Wildflowers sat on the table. The table itself was fashioned from splintered wood – the same wood used in the construction of the four-poster bed. Then the people in the vision vanished.

She heard someone shout, "Anna! Anna!" Instantly, it was twilight and in the doorframe, with a burning red sun as backlight, stood the lone silhouette of a woman.

Robin awoke to find herself in near panic. She looked about the room now illuminated only by a night-light. The house was still; a dog barked in the distance. Her heart continued to pound as she lay on her back staring at the ceiling until the curtains revealed the true morning twilight.

- 15 -

MORNING ARRIVES

She dressed and opened the double doors that led from the bedroom to the porch. Wisteria adorned the porch columns. The flowering plant grew far too quickly and covered any object that was stationary including pine trees and abandon houses. So thick were its leaves and blossoms that trees often died from lack of sunshine.

The purple wisteria blossoms enriched the morning air with their aroma. The scent of wild honeysuckle blended with the blossoms to create the perfect morning blend of natural odors. In the center of the porch was a modern plastic outdoor table surrounded by four matching white chairs. The centerpiece consisted of freshly cut wildflowers placed in a crystal Waterford vase. Glasses of fresh orange juice sat on the table as well as a pot of coffee warmed by a paraffin flame.

The Professor soon entered from the adjoining parlor doors and joined her on the porch. "Please be seated." He pulled the chair out for her. "Now Robin, tell me how your night was," he said quietly. "I hope that you slept soundly after such a day of travel. The night woods can be filled with sounds since wild animals often come out in the darkness to hunt for prey."

Robin did not know how to respond to his question. She did not know him well enough to be so honest as to describe her feelings at that moment. Should she mention the vision in the mirror or the terrifying dream she had experienced? Was this the time to question him about the mannequin? Should she ask if there were panthers in the nearby woods?

"Professor, it must be my imagination, but I keep having the feeling that someone is watching me."

"It is just a feeling I assure you," the Professor said as he took her hand and held it briefly.

"I hope that you are right," replied Robin.

"Who was Anna?" she asked herself again. She did not know a living person with that name. There were so many questions. At first, she thought it would be rude to bother him for answers to them all. She felt, however, a great need to discuss the events that had just transpired with him.

She spoke softly, almost confidentially as though others were present, "Professor, I had a dream last night that was very real. In the dream, someone was calling the name, 'Anna.' It's strange because I do not know anyone with that name. At one point, I thought I heard a woman crying." She chose not to mention the silhouette of the woman in the doorway.

The Professor looked inquisitively at her. "Robin, you must have forgotten. The main character in the outline that I sent to you is named Anna. The reason why I picked that name is of some interest. When a former tenant and his wife were living in the house, the wife would often hear voices very much like what my mother described. One day when my tenant's husband was at work, she heard a woman weeping. She asked the unseen person her name. A feminine voice said something like 'Annie' or perhaps 'Anna.' Immediately the tenant called me and asked if either name meant anything to me.

"Just moments before, I had typed the name *Anna* in the outline of my proposed manuscript about the house. I later sent the outline to you. Probably you remember that name from having read my submission. Sometimes it is very difficult to explain coincidences."

ߺ

The Professor then mentioned that he needed to spend the remainder of the day on his university's campus. He had an afternoon and an early evening class to teach. In addition, he indicated that he had two morning meetings that he was obligated to attend.

"Robin, I hope that you don't mind my being gone so much today. There is food in the refrigerator for you. You already know where the wine is kept. Please feel free to use my other car if you like. The keys are on top of my desk. I look forward to our creative writing session this evening when I return." He spoke with a strong regional accent, having failed once again to address the completed manuscript.

Robin recognized his need to work and assured him to take his time for she had plenty to read. Soon, she heard his VW Bug crank up and watched him descend down the hill into the pines that lined the long driveway to the county road below. The house whispered once more in creaks and moans.

As the Professor drove, he thought about the manuscript. The basic thesis of the outline he sent to Robin involved the arrival of a young woman at Mt. Ebal with the single purpose of writing a story with him. The subject was to be the history of Mt. Ebal. Since the house had escaped destruction on numerous occasions, he thought about adding a storyline that might generate some interest. After all, the website about the house being destroyed by the tornado had generated over 4,000 hits in two weeks. With Robin being an author and a well-established publisher, he wanted to bounce ideas off her as they wrote. He envisioned the visit as a series of sessions in which their discussions about the events related to the house could be interwoven into the fabric of a story. The only thing missing was an interesting storyline that connected all events together.

The Professor now, however, marveled at how the outline of the story was no longer a work of fiction, but perhaps one of fact. He once more wondered what the manuscript really contained since he had only briefly glanced at it. Had Robin written about their meeting before her arrival in an attempt to deliberately control the sequence of events?

In the deepest recesses of his thoughts, he wondered if perhaps the manuscript itself were a blueprint of events that were to transpire and they themselves merely characters in a completed literary work. He knew he should have read more of the manuscript, but instead had put it down quickly, hesitant to confront Robin that evening regarding its authorship. Perhaps later, when his rational nature had returned, he would study it in greater detail.

His early morning class went fine. He very much appreciated that the students demonstrated a respectful interest in the class. He did not like being challenged by undergraduates who, through the use of communication technologies, including the Internet, were often more up-to-date than he was. While he had exiled himself to Mt. Ebal, they had joined the global community. They traveled at T1 speed while he was still using a dial-up modem.

The early evening classes often went less well. The graduate students showed declining interest. Many had full-time jobs and families to occupy their passion and time.

He could generate involvement at the beginning of the semester, but by midterm, their interest had dwindled as their texting during classes increased. Even he knew that his lectures had become dull and without meaningful application to their busy professional lives. He thought seriously about letting them go early or even at the break. The decision was made for him when one of the class members raised her hand.

"What do these assignments have to do with the subject matter of this class? They aren't even in the syllabus."

Stunned, he did not know how to respond at first. After a thoughtful pause, he said, "Young lady, I can assure you that they are relevant to the class or I would not have assigned them. Remember, I am looking from the perspective of the whole course content. You, however, to paraphrase Saint Paul, see in part and thus only know in part. The relevancy of the assignments will become clear at the conclusion of the semester."

"I still...." she responded.

"The class is dismissed for the evening," the Professor replied.

cs

Robin leisurely spent a few moments looking at the tall bookcase in the parlor. It had been constructed with great detail. The dark walnut-stained shelves were supported by fluted columns that held in place an elaborate entablature depicting a series of hand-carved cherubs, their stares focused upon the parlor guest below. Against the entablature was fastened a ladder that could be easily slid across the top portion of the bookcase, allowing the highest shelf to be reached.

One book at the top of the bookcase jutted out, capturing Robin's interest. It had heavy leather binding with gold-edged pages and appeared older and more of a collectible than the rest of the volumes.

She positioned the ladder so as to retrieve it. But no matter how she stood on tiptoes, she could barely touch it. She did notice the title; it was simply *R. F.*

"It must be a diary or a ledger," she thought. There was so much to see and do that she quickly lost interest in obtaining the bound volume that rested high upon the bookcase. It now peered down at her like the carved cherubs that adorned the entablature.

She then turned around on the ladder and noticed that the opposing front room door was open. Robin did not recall it being open when she entered the library.

There before her was the seated mannequin reflected in the mirror. Its motionless eyes appeared to be looking up at her. For a moment Robin's legs felt weak. She held tightly to the ladder as small beads of sweat appeared on her forehead. She conscientiously placed one leg beneath the other, one rung at a time.

"I have got to get down from this ladder before I fall," she said out loud to the vacant room. Her heart rate increased. The beats sounded loudly in her ears as the perspiration beaded on her forehead.

Rather than remain in the parlor, she quickly left to sit on the porch swing. The odors were very pleasant and the sounds of bees and other insects were reminders that spring was arriving very early this year. She thought of one of the descriptive poems that the Professor had sent her earlier.

A Moment in a Country Garden

Sunflowers border my father's garden,

Summer cloud the only shade.
The soil is soft and warm beneath my feet;
Gourd-dipped water awaits the heat of day.

Wild bees fly freely among the blooming plants.
Corn's tasseled hair turns golden in morning light.
Tomatoes grow sunset red in the warmed soil,
Cucumber to mother's chow-chow and pickle jar.
Okra stings the hands as melons expand.

Cicada sings in midsummer's choir.
Cut worm, grub worm and other intruders join the feast uninvited.
Lady Bugs and Dragon Flies dine upon the garden table.

A summer garden fills with the blooming of life.
There is neither sadness here nor media's blaring report.
Though column demands, no report to be made,
no rushes amongst marigold and corn.
A summer breeze, a gathering storm,
delight the twilight of the fading day.
Sleep made rich by rural contentment profound.

I looked at him, my father, with fear and respect.
Unreachable man, skin darkened by Texas sun,
You sleep now in earth well-tended.
I did not know it then,
but the sun, the garden and my father cared for me.

The Professor did not seem capable of writing anything so descriptive and at the same time so gentle. It was as though two men had invited her to Mt. Ebal. One was a somber historian while the other was a poet of compassion.

She observed a small fox that entered the fringes of the yard only to dart back into the pines and undergrowth. Doves and crows chattered away in the forest. The surrounding woods and undergrowth were made much thicker after the tornado that had, a decade before, destroyed the mature trees.

Abruptly she heard the noise of a very large animal making its way through the dense undergrowth. She stared in the direction of the noise, expecting a deer or turkey to appear, perhaps even the panther that made the scream-like noise the night before.

The noise grew louder as the animal ventured towards the house. No animal, however, appeared. The woods were suddenly silent. The locusts that had stopped their shrill sounds soon began their chorus again. Only the slight movement of the undergrowth indicated the large animal's presence. It was as though it had stopped abruptly just beyond her sight. Now only the faint sounds of the animal's movements remained within the dark undergrowth as it pushed the brush aside, unseen.

"I know that Appalachia has black bears. Perhaps it is one. I must ask the Professor if they venture this far south."

෫

Somewhat unnerved by the natural sounds produced within the early springwoods, Robin moved back to the parlor. After all, she was from the city. She did not know what typical or atypical noises to expect and what visitors from the forest she might unwittingly encounter.

She enjoyed the comfortable fireside chair. The footstool added to the support of her legs. A slight breeze sounded from the chimney top. Soon unidentifiable chatter was heard coming from the direction of the chimney.

Robin remembered the Professor's words about his somewhat similar experiences in Texas:

If you sat quietly near the fireplace on a warm summer night at the farmhouse, you could hear what sounds like a room full of people in casual conversation. It was similar to the indistinguishable chatter of a New Orleans' restaurant. Some evenings my family would invite company to listen to the sounds. In that the farmhouse was more than a mile from the nearest neighbor, such chatter was even more unusual. Occasionally, a distinct word could be heard or even the sound of a trumpet or piano. The unusual sounds soon took the character of a parlor game, as guests would add their interpretations to what was being heard. The farmhouse now sits empty. Perhaps the great room with its chatter is silent now.

"It must be the wind that I keep hearing in the chimney," she thought. Through the antique windowpanes, she viewed the yard once more noting the distortions that the antique glass provided. Robin could still see the direction from which the sound she had heard in the undergrowth came from.

In the general area, she noted a section of growth that appeared to be darker than other areas and yet did not have a defined shape. At first curious, then frightened, she reasoned that it must be a collection of small cedars or perhaps the trunk of a decayed tree. The dark object, however, now appeared to be that of a large black bear waiting – waiting for her to leave the safety of the house.

The image within the forest bothered her enough that she looked away from the view of the yard and immediately looked back towards the fireplace mantel studying the various artifacts that had been placed upon it. Behind her, the mannequin sat facing the opposite direction towards the silent television set that still showed only static and the occasional flickering image of an unidentified person in the reflective surface of the antique mirror.

"At least, the Professor had bothered to cut the volume off before he left," she faintly said aloud allowing the sound of her own voice to provide the only comfort to her.

ଏ

Within the Professor's house, she experienced a familiar feeling of being trapped. Her teenage years had been spent in New England where her parents had owned a large house that dated back to the 1700s. The house had at one time been the centerpiece of a large farm. During the

1950s, however, suburban sprawl had reached the garden fence. It was a large saltbox type house with low ceilings and a fireplace designed for mid-eighteenth century cooking. The walls were unpainted and darkened by the soot of countless fires. It too had its share of strange noises and unseen imaginary guests.

Her parents preferred not to use electricity for light and heat. Instead, candles provided light while heat came from the large brick fireplaces that adorned each room. They felt that it was more in harmony with nature and enhanced the purity of the soul.

Her father was a physician who often was called to the local hospital at night to oversee his patients who were recovering from surgery. As a child, she dreaded the all too familiar phone calls he would receive. Her mother had died several years before in an automobile accident. Whenever she was alone at night and heard an unfamiliar sound, she would stand in the open yard until her father returned. She preferred to stand as far away from the trees and bushes as possible. Her father would then reproach her for being outside. He felt strongly that being inside was much safer. He always reminded her, before leaving for the hospital, where his loaded .45 caliber pistol was kept. Yet she never opened his desk drawer to retrieve it for she felt that what frightened her the most could not be stopped by a mere weapon. Regardless of her father's pleas and his objective reasoning, she felt more secure outside the locked doors than within. She believed that outside she could outrun whatever was threatening her, yet her rational reasoning said otherwise.

Her fear of being trapped inside might have stemmed from, at least she thought, a terrible dream that she had as a child; a dream in which a woman without a face was standing above her bed humming a nondescript tune. When she awoke startled from the dream, she could smell a strong scent of lavender. She felt that if she could flee from the odor, she would be safe. It was the same odor that now permeated the parlor of the Professor's house yet not as strong as in her childhood memory.

She thought silently, "Even with the footstool, my legs hurt from sitting down so much. I need to walk some. If I remember correctly, the Professor mentioned that the house adjoined Mt. Ebal cemetery. Perhaps I can spend some time reading the gravestones. It is such a beautiful day that I need to be in the sunlight. It should cheer me up."

She was determined not to let her fears keep her a captive within the house. She reasoned that the forest sounds were from birds and small animals. Robin knew that she had let her imagination run wild, and now she felt ashamed of herself. She said out loud to both herself and to the house, "If it is death that I fear, then I am most foolish for we must all cease to be. But not today!"

She picked up a walking stick from the hall tree. She noticed that the mirror was missing on the piece of furniture. Robin wondered, "Why no mirror here when the bathroom and the rest of the house have numerous ornate mirrors?"

☃

Robin then proceeded down the tree-lined driveway, not looking back towards the house or in the direction from whence the sound within the woods had previously come. The sun felt good upon her bare shoulders while a large flower-adorned hat protected her face from its rays. Adding to the pleasure of the moment, she was at last free from the scent of lavender.

The walking stick was heavy with its ornate American Indian carvings of sacred animals. At the top of the stick was an intricate carving of a bear standing on its hind legs as if ready to attack a prey. "I shall not be afraid of shadows," she said out loud. She then looked down the shaft to see where the walking stick was made. There was, however, no country of origin or other identifying marks to be seen. She assumed that it must have been hand-carved by a local artisan. Despite the Trail of Tears, some of the descendants of the Creek and Cherokee Indians still lived in the vicinity.

- 16 -
THE STRANGERS

Mt. Ebal cemetery dated from 1832. The church that adjoined the cemetery had been rebuilt twice since that date due to two tornadoes that followed the same path a hundred years apart. The cemetery lay upon the slope of a hill that fronted onto Mt. Ebal. The graveyard, however, could not be seen from the house due to the thick wall of trees that separated the two. Like the storm before it, the last tornado that destroyed the house also destroyed the church and did considerable damage to the upright tombstones within the burial grounds.

As she walked along Mt. Ebal road, wind blew through the treetops, making the pines talk in a whisper. As she approached the cemetery, she noticed three people working around a grave in the distance. It was comforting to her to know that people were so physically close even if they were but strangers. She could not see their faces, but they appeared to be two men and a woman. The woman was wearing an old-fashioned bonnet. Robin had not seen a bonnet like it since she saw her grandmother wearing one many years ago while working in the family garden. The three people were busy weeding a burial plot and did not look in her direction.

At the entryway, she stopped to look at some interesting grave markers covered in green moss. She bent over to pick a yellow flower. She held it in her hand while examining the brilliance of its color. A small mountain stream provided just enough moisture in the air to keep the moss alive and vividly green upon the gray marble markers.

As she read the stones, many of the earliest graves showed the date of death as being 1863. The War Between the States was being waged in all of its ferocity. Alabama had contributed more than her share of young men and boys to the cause. This fact could be a possible answer to the common date of death shown on so many of the lichen-marked stones.

Robin also reasoned that in that time period, it was not unusual for epidemics to occur. The Professor told her that his own grandmother had died in 1913 as a result of a typhoid fever epidemic that struck rural north Texas. She had drunk untreated cistern water at a friend's house. She languished with a burning fever for three days. Even though her husband had medical training and was a registered pharmacist, he could not save her. For days her family stood by her as they watched her body grow weaker and weaker until she died in the heat of an August day.

The Professor related how his father only remembered her as a four-year-old would sitting in his mother's lap while playing with her gold necklace. He could not remember any other detail about her. The Professor had mentioned how often he thought about her unattended grave in a small Texas cemetery named "Lanora." There was no other family buried nearby which accentuated the loneliness of her grave. It was as if she had never existed even though the Professor carried her genetic markings.

⅓

Robin looked in the direction of the three people who had been weeding the grave plot only to notice that they were no longer there. In that she was at the entryway to the cemetery, she wondered why they had not walked past her. She thought also that they must have been local since they had not driven to the cemetery. Perhaps they had exited through a path that could not be seen from the entryway.

She walked towards the gravesite that they had been weeding. As she neared the approximate location where the three strangers had been working, none of the graves appeared to have been weeded or cleared of any brush. Goldenrods and young saplings grew around each of the graves. Their headstones lay horizontal upon the ground as a result of the violent wind that had occurred ten years previously.

The inscriptions were now barely discernible upon the aged stones. It was apparent from the markings that two of the people buried there were Confederate officers while the third grave belonged to an unrelated woman. They all died in 1863.

She traced the names by using the powder in her purse. The first grave bore the name Phillip Renfro, Colonel, CSA, March 27, 1863. The second grave was that of a woman, Annie Fuller Finch, March 27, 1863. The third grave belonged to a Lt. Gregory F. Haynes, CSA. He too died on March 27, 1863. The significance of the dates was not lost on Robin as tomorrow was, in fact, March 27.

She sat down upon an overturned marker while staring into the darkening forest. Lengthening shadows crawled among the stones as a mosquito hummed loudly in her ear. Startled, she looked at her watch. "I can't believe it, time has flown too quickly. It is already early evening." Perhaps she had fallen asleep while resting upon the stone? No other explanation could account for such a rapid passage of time.

- 17 -
RETURN

As she ascended Mt. Ebal's driveway, the Professor came down to greet her. "Robin, I was worried when I came home and you were not here," he said in a voice that conveyed sincerity. "Then it dawned on me," he continued, "that since the car was still parked in the driveway, you might have walked to the cemetery. The weather has been so nice and the scent of flowers so strong that I imagined the aroma of honeysuckle led you to the gates of Mt. Ebal. You know, it is an interesting cemetery with many links to the Old South."

Robin was breathing heavily as they ascended to the porch of the house. She paused, looking back in the direction of the cemetery and at the crests of the nearby mountains. Rain crows sounded as she turned towards the darkened interior of the house.

"Before we set up to write, let's sit on the porch and have a drink," suggested the Professor. He soon arrived with bourbon, water and ice. The rising moon turned pale as it ascended further above the ridge top. The air continued to feel unseasonably warm even as moonlight glistened off the nearby magnolia leaves. Her earlier apprehension vanished in the pleasant conversation of the evening.

"Please let me reiterate once more how very nice it is of you to come to Mt. Ebal. As you may have guessed, I do get lonely here," the Professor said. "My work is very important to me, but it is no longer enough. There is always a remote feeling that something here or in my life is not yet completed. I know that upon my death, no one will remember me. Even when academic buildings bear the name of a contributor or a university president, it is not long before they are bulldozed into the earth and the name of the one that gave so much is forgotten. It frightens me to think that to retire is to be forgotten."

"You are still very young for a professor. I don't think you need to worry about retirement just yet," she said with a smile.

"Perhaps you are right, I should not worry about the future. I just know what must soon be," he said sincerely.

◌ঌ

The Professor had prepared a meal of fried chicken, corn on the cob, mashed potatoes, fried green tomatoes and fried okra. Pickled green beans provided a tart taste to the abundant platters of food. Tetley Sweet Tea and lemon were also served.

While those that live in the north might choose to dwell upon the ill effects that such a meal might have upon one's health, none could deny the excellent taste that such a table produced. The fresh vegetables and chicken had come from either the field or the lush garden of Mt. Ebal.

Since the evening continued to be warm, they ate on the porch. The only light came from the moon and the three candles on the table. Red wine followed the tea and was poured freely into large crystal wine glasses. Whippoorwills sounded throughout the moonlit forest. The night air continued to embrace them in warmth.

An owl then sounded loudly from the forest, returning their attention to the writing of the book. The Professor looked at her and smiled. "I guess it is time to move back into the parlor and begin writing. Soon there will be a chill upon the night. After all, that is why you made the trip to Mt. Ebal. I hope that something original will come from our work," he said in a soft voice.

He knew that creativity had passed from him. Rejection slips from professional journals were pasted like sticky notes on his bookcase. Reminders to bring a fresh perspective to already trite and overwritten subjects came from publishers. He had also written a book of poetry that a close relative, upon reading it, only replied, "It was nice."

Robin felt it inappropriate to once more mention that the manuscript was already complete and that no edits, including additions, were needed. Yet, it would be pleasant to imagine other events that could be added into the context of the document. She had, after all, been flattered by his invitation for her to contribute to the project.

☓

The Professor had previously moved a handmade table into the parlor. Its planks revealed the unique patterns of rough-cut wood that appeared in small sections through the torn tablecloth. The tabletop also bore lettering and other symbols. The messages had been carved deeply into the wood, but could not be read unless the cloth covering was completely removed. Robin's curiosity made her want to look beneath the linen shroud.

The Professor had placed laptops at each end of the table. They were connected to bulky extension cords that dangled from brass wall plates. The seats were uncomfortable, straight-backed wicker bottom chairs that were intended to be painted, but instead had aged with rain and sun exposure. It was most probable that they had served as his front porch furniture. The fact that they might have also been aged on another porch was a distinct possibility, considering his love for trade days.

Robin and the Professor sat facing one another like opponents in a medieval tournament in which weapons had already been selected. At either end of the rectangular table, they waited. "Now remind me how we are to write this story," Robin said. Her mind now belabored by the wine and full meal.

"That is not a problem." He smiled. "I will tell the story from my perspective – the aged professor who entices the younger woman to come to Mt. Ebal while you are to provide your own view of what has happened so far and what might happen to the two individuals. We will keep the concept simple." He continued, "We will be writing in a stream of consciousness style."

"We must be careful that it does not turn out to be another *Ulysses*." She laughed. "So," she added, "the story is really about us. How we react to the house and to each other, a very different plot to say the least. I assume that when we draw a blank, we can drink more wine." She smiled coquettishly.

The Professor intended to mention several events, then ask her to respond to them, adding details that he might overlook.

"As you know, both Mt. Ebal and my home in Texas have had very parallel experiences. Sometimes when we do not listen to one another, whether it is a priest, lover or friend, tragedy can result. An old college roommate called me one night. He said that his son and daughter-in-law needed a place to stay while he worked in the oil fields. I agreed to rent the house to them as a favor. Within a short period of time, his daughter-in-law began to hear voices.

"She frequently called his son at work telling him that she heard people talking. The son, however, ignored her concerns. Like my mother had told me before regarding Mt. Ebal, his wife informed him that they needed to move from the house or something terrifying would happen.

"The son, however, continued to ignore her pleas. The more weeks passed, the more frequent her calls became. He often had to leave work to drive to the house. In fact, he had lost more than one job because of the repeated calls and the necessity to take time off.

"One day she called saying she had slit her wrists; a task that she had indeed accomplished. Had he not arrived in time, she would have bled to death. She could no longer handle the fear that had accumulated within her. After that, both of them abruptly left the house. They left the beds unmade. No clothing was taken by either one of them in their hasty departure. It was as though they had simply walked out the door to run an errand.

"His son also mentioned that she was particularly afraid of one room. One day he returned home to find the door to that room barricaded with furniture. When asked, she said that she had not moved the furniture in front of the door. She also stated that items of her clothing frequently went missing from the closet under the stairwell."

The Professor continued, "I have since spent a lot of time thinking about this. They didn't even bother to turn down the air-conditioner thermostat from 55 degrees before fleeing the house. It was August and the temperature was well over 100. The units ran for two months before I had time to visit the house and see what had actually happened. I had to repaint the rooms due to the damage caused by condensation. Even the vents had rusted.

"Robin, as you recall, the photograph that was taken at the farmhouse shows a ghostlike image appearing through a burned-out window. After the photograph was made, I had that portion of the house destroyed. Perhaps it is possible that the image moved into the room just off the kitchen. Obviously, the presence survived the fire.

"It is odd that she feared the only room in the house that was left original. After the fire, the other rooms had their sheet rock removed as well as the remnants of ancient wallpaper that still clung to the wooden walls. The walls of that room, however, had never been covered.

"Within the room that she feared, there was a painted name and date, *Otis Weems, Year 1915*. Other tenants and owners were to later write their names on the wall. I did not know many of the people whose autographs had been left upon the bare wood. I assume that many of these individuals are now dead."

Robin did not react to his comments. To admit that a person must forewarn others of an image or presence is to admit that spirits exist, something Robin was not yet prepared to acknowledge. She found little or no comfort in a fictional faith. Robin did admit to herself that the Bible was a masterful work of fiction, nothing more.

Robin then asked her host, "Professor, would you mind cutting off the mannequin's television set? The flicker is reflected on the windows and it's causing my mind to wander to less than pleasant thoughts. I keep seeing barely defined images from the set across the windowpanes." She took another sip of the sweet, locally grown muscadine wine.

"You mentioned being alone as a possible motivator for inviting me here. I assume that this is not a case of entrapment." She smiled. "That is, however, an interesting idea. A plot built upon that concept might take us in many directions."

The Professor replied in a serious tone, "I have learned to be alone. Yes, I do want to be loved; to feel desired and wanted by someone. I am very much aware, however, that we live no longer than these wildflowers I have placed upon the table. They are beautiful tonight, but will have wilted by the morning sun. I have often feared that my free verse, or narrative if you will, offers the reader no more than a dream state. How does one awaken desire that sleeps within the heart? Does love not die like the body?"

Robin reacted after a paused. "Perhaps you need to consider that I too may be without anyone as well. Truly it was, at least in part, loneliness that brought me here."

Robin knew that she had not been attracted to the Professor. She was a pilgrim walking upon sharp stones. Robin remembered the flower she had picked in the cemetery. She reached into her pocket and gently removed it. Now wilted, its beauty no longer remained. She placed it gently on the tablecloth.

To her, love could not exist without emotional pain. She often thought, "Why love if it only prepares you to be betrayed?"

She remembered her own recent marriage with both sadness and bitterness. Robin's husband, after they had made love and fallen asleep, awakened her. "Robin, I am no longer emotionally involved with you. I feel nothing regarding our relationship. Ruth at the office fills all of my needs. She understands me, something you never did." Since that night, she had fought against her natural instinct to feel anger, an emotion not easily restrained.

The Professor continued, "You are young and very attractive, educated and interesting. Perhaps your being alone is by choice and not one of circumstance. Unlike you, I am alone because of age and my own bitterness that lives deep within me. I am the product of the storm, a continuation of my moment in hell."

The Professor looked towards the mannequin. "Let's start our in-depth discussion, related to the house, with this fact. One thing that I only mentioned briefly was that after the tornado, I was able to look at the original construction techniques used in the building of the house. Timbers were strewn about the yard. Dentil molding rested in small heaps of debris. It was apparent that square nails and pegs were used in its construction; earth had been put inside the walls for insulation and horsehair was used in the plaster. These building techniques were typical of very early building in the Deep South. This method of building ended with the close of the War Between the States.

"The only exception to early construction techniques was the one hall wall that collapsed into the adjacent original wall. It was tongue-in-groove construction. I also noted that round-headed nails had been used in its building. I would think that indicated that the original wall itself had been replaced after the initial construction and certainly following the War Between the States. Much of the other wood was hand-hewn and not millwork.

"I don't know why the original wall was replaced. Perhaps a fire or a storm damaged it. I know that when I repaired the fire damage to my farmhouse in Texas, some walls were removed and others added without touching the exterior walls or flooring.

"When the Palm Sunday storm occurred, I found some walls standing adjacent to other rooms that were now entirely missing from the house. Often horrific events do not have a pattern to them and, therefore, defy our ability to ascertain what has transpired. Perhaps a series of tragic events explain the imbalance of the house," said the Professor as he switched from hot tea to bourbon.

Robin attempted to react to his thoughts. From the corner of her eyes, however, she noted the reflection of the fire on the mannequin's cypress hand. Rather than wood, her hand appeared now to be porcelain. How else could the flames reflect so clearly upon it? In addition, she noticed for the first time that several large mirrors hung on the walls including a full-length one mounted in a portable frame that rested upon a heavily built oak easel.

"Were these mirrors here before I left for my walk to the cemetery?" she wondered. "Of course, the dimly lit room would not have highlighted reflections within it as the firelight now does."

Robin then noted, "Uh, you are correct in your statement regarding the significance of the obviously dissimilar construction periods. To say, however, that something horrific occurred here is to overlook the fact that this could have been simply a remodeling effort on the part of one or more generations of owners. Didn't Greek Revival eventually metamorphose into Gothic? After all, when the Civil War ended, styles and tastes changed dramatically."

She continued, "By the way, Professor, is the weather this time of year always so warm as it is now? I noticed that many plants are blooming and how good the air smells with their scents. Honeysuckle is everywhere in bloom in the cemetery. It has such a sweet smell. I have promised myself to cut some tomorrow and place it in a vase within my room."

The Professor looked at her and replied, "I too love the smell of honeysuckle and also the gardenias that are now blooming in the garden. My favorite scent, however, is that of lavender."

He wanted very much to place his hand upon hers. He hesitated in making such a bold move. "This is unusually early for such warm and unsettled weather. We have had several very warm days, high humidity and rain. I think that all of this has contributed to a very early spring. Of course, Blackberry winter will follow with a few cooler days. The fruit trees will then suffer the most since their blossoms and early buds are very sensitive to temperature change."

"Unfortunately all of these factors will result in a more violent and tornado-prone season," the Professor added as a downdraft stirred the flames within the fireplace. As a result, copious amounts of smoke and swirling ash entered the room.

❣

As their discussion about Mt. Ebal continued, an early spring storm once more formed resulting in a rain that pounded the windowpanes in violent burst followed by summit lightning. The house shook in a rude awakening.

The Professor thought how, after moving the house to the top of the hill known as Mt. Ebal, he had taken pleasure in watching the streaks of horizontal lighting and those opportunistic moments when lighting would appear to travel from one mountain top to another.

His mind returned to the present building storm. The hall clock could be heard above the sound of the rain upon the metal roof. The downdrafts continued to create a firestorm as burning ashes swirled about, rose and returned to the hearth. The lights flickered for a moment; then the room appeared darker as though the power was starting to falter.

Suddenly, the room was dark except for the fire and the lightning outside. The power had failed completely which was usually the result of a tree having fallen across the lines. Power could be restored immediately or it might not be until morning. The Professor fumbled about on his desktop feeling for matches. Having found them, he lit one on his way to the kerosene lamp that sat upon the mantelpiece for just such an emergency.

"Oh, there we are. Light at last," the triumphant Professor said. The flickering flame made his eyes appear more recessed, with dark shadows being prominent in the uncertain light. It was noticeable that his hand shook as he carried the lamp to the table; exaggerated by the shadow-box image of his frame upon the wall.

Robin then continued the conversation, "I saw some people in the cemetery this afternoon that you might know. They were working around a few graves. Two Confederate officers and a woman are buried near the location where they happened to be weeding. When I walked over to the spot where they had been standing, they were gone and no sign of anyone disturbing the weeds or wildflowers was apparent. It was like they were there and a moment later they were not present. They should have passed right by me on their way out of the cemetery. I noticed that on the side of the cemetery where they were working, there is a creek with steep banks and thick undergrowth made up of blackberry bushes and honeysuckle. I doubt if anyone would choose that route over leaving the cemetery through the gate. If they used the main path, they would have walked right past me. They just literally vanished." Her statement proffered a question as much as factual information.

The Professor looked very concerned. "What was the name on the woman's gravestone?"

"It was difficult to read but I believe that it was Annie Fuller Finch. I think it was odd that all three of the people buried there had died on the same date in 1863. I also noticed several other very old markers with the same date of death. What could have happened on that date? They were not all Confederate soldiers."

"Robin, I really don't know. I understand that there were several small battles fought not far from here. It was not unusual for civilians to be caught in the crossfire. In fact, a Confederate recruitment camp was just down the road from Mt. Ebal on what is now Seven Springs Road. For all I know, it may have been attacked during the War. Many of the people who live in the immediate vicinity are Confederate descendants."

The Professor spoke as though giving a lecture. "The Baptist church that adjoins the cemetery was first established in 1832. It is also possible that a well was contaminated with typhoid. That disease kills very quickly."

Robin could no longer keep her question to herself. "Were these mirrors in the room before I left for my walk? I just don't remember them being here at that time." She recalled the mirrors in the bathroom, yet these were different. Their frames were similar yet they were larger, thicker in wood and dark gold in color. The mirrors that she now saw appeared to be even older than those in the bathroom with more imperfections and distortions.

The Professor answered after a brief, thoughtful pause. "You are correct, I put the mirrors in the parlor when I returned home today. I had stored them under the house. I had hoped that they might add to the room. I am sorry if my placing them here has disturbed you. I just don't have anywhere else to put them. As I mentioned earlier, I am a collector and the items I enjoy collecting the most are antique mirrors, their unique reflected images fascinate me. I know that this must be a strange hobby to you.

"Besides, since we are writing about the house and the past, however distant or unclear it may be, I thought that the mirrors might serve to assist us. As I mentioned before, there is a medical doctor in White Plains, Alabama that has written several books about contacting the dead. Even though he lives in a nearby community, I have only talked to him on the phone and only after my own experience in the vortex of the tornado. He felt that I had a near-death experience."

"Why? It sounds to me like you had a very realistic experience, all things considered," stated Robin.

The Professor replied, "That is true except that I did not hear or feel anything and was in a state of grace."

Robin asked, "Grace?"

"Yes, by that I mean, acceptance with profound peace. The doctor mentioned in one of his books that ancient peoples at their temple sites attempted to contact the dead through the use of reflective surfaces such as water or semiprecious stones. Often these reflective sites were the centerpieces of oracles. While I don't expect us to be able to contact the dead, I do think that the mirrors will add another dimension to our writing. Sometimes when looking into a mirror, we see more than ourselves."

The mirrors made the parlor look much larger. Each mirror, depending on its position, reflected the glow of the kerosene lantern as well as the flames within the fireplace. The reflections emphasized the pallor of the mannequin's skin. Some mirrors contained reflections of other mirrors that seemed to repeat the image into infinity.

Occasionally, lightning would also be reflected from their surfaces. One especially strong lightning flash illuminated the yard, causing Robin to glance in the direction of the strike. There in the yard were three motionless indistinct figures. Robin looked away in terror, and then into the mirror, suddenly realizing that she was not seeing the mannequin. Her heart pounded just as another flash lit the yard to reveal that it was free of any visitors. When she looked back into the mirror again, the mannequin was just as it had previously been that evening.

Robin looked at the Professor and said, "I must have drunk too much wine or perhaps the food is not agreeing with me, but I thought that I just saw three people in the yard! Perhaps the most unusual thing is that when I first looked back into the mirror, the image of the mannequin was not there."

The Professor looked at her and smiled. "I don't think anyone would be standing outside in this storm. Sometimes in a thunderstorm, dark cedars of various heights appear like people standing. At night, it is very difficult to judge distance. I am sure that is what you saw, just some trees, nothing more.

"I imagine that the flash blinded your eyes for just a moment. Didn't you see the mannequin again once your eyes adjusted to the light of the kerosene lamp? I can assure you that the mannequin did not venture out into the storm." He walked over to the mannequin and patted it on the shoulder. "See?" he added. "It is just where I placed it weeks ago."

Robin, however, noticed that water had dripped onto the wooden floor beside the mannequin's seat. Perhaps, the Professor's hand was wet from holding his wine glass. "No, there are too many drops of water on the floor for that to be possible," she reasoned.

The Professor, while appearing to be very calm and self-assured, was uneasy himself. He tried not to allow his shock to be seen when he felt the outer garment of the mannequin and noticed that it was soaked with water. Being a scientific man, more acquainted with mathematical rules than with superstitions, he reasoned that the roof must be leaking directly above the mannequin's rocker. He would have to remember to call a roofer in the morning. He also thought that it would be better to move the mannequin away from the drip after Robin had gone to bed. He saw no advantage in alarming her for something as common as a leaking roof.

In his desire to save money after the house's destruction, the Professor had cut costs by not having the roofer put decking under the metal roof. Instead the builder screwed the metal sheets directly into a series of parallel 1- by 8-inch wooden rafters. He remembered that no one thought the house could be rebuilt, including him, and that the original plan was to make it into a small barn. Besides, the lack of decking would intensify the soothing sound of a winter rain.

"Robin, as you know, first impressions are lasting ones. What are your feelings towards Mt. Ebal now that you have been here for almost two full days?" asked the Professor. Outside, the rain continued while limbs of nearby trees scraped against the metal roof like wild animals seeking entry into their den.

"Professor, I really believe that this house is more than simply an old wooden structure. It seems to be communicating with me in a way that I do not yet understand. I still have not gotten over the very vivid dream from last night. It was so absolutely real. In addition, the three figures in the cemetery, I must admit, have really troubled me. Even at a distance, their clothing looked so different. It is as if they too are trying to communicate with me. I don't know why they didn't approach me. Have you seen any sightings that you cannot explain while living here?" she questioned.

"In that it may help with the writing of this book, yes, I saw a person that looked very much like the mannequin on campus. I now must assume that a student just happened to look like her or at least I thought so at the time." After taking a sip of his bourbon, he continued, "It was in the administration building. I was walking up a staircase when I noticed a young woman descending. The large window behind her at first created a silhouette of her image. As she descended, I got only a brief glimpse of her face. At first I wondered where I had seen her before. Her face was pallid, her hair long and black, and her clothes were very simple. It was perhaps her intense stare that bothered me – for when I said hello, as is my custom to greet students even those unknown to me, she did not respond. She continued to look straight ahead, her eyes unmoving. When it finally dawned on me that she looked very much like the mannequin, it was too late. I even walked rapidly to each of the two side entryways in my attempt to locate her. She just simply was not there. I guess what struck me most was how cold the stairwell felt after she had passed by me.

"I admit that I saw her again, or at least I think so, only two weeks ago at the community center. I was walking on the raised track above the basketball court when I noticed a young woman walking in front of me. She stopped before a window that looked out onto a field and waved. At first I thought nothing of it and walked swiftly by. After an additional lap, I glanced at the field, but there was no one there, only grass and distant trees. Finally, I stopped and asked her,

'Have you found what you are looking for?' I know it was a strange question to ask a stranger, but she replied, 'Yes, he is there.' I continued on my lap. When I looked back, she was gone."

The Professor did not mention the other encounter that forced him off the highway. For a brief moment, he recalled fighting to keep his automobile from either hitting the bridge abutment or crashing into the stream below. Surely the moment of panic had caused him to imagine seeing the mannequin's face behind the darkened windows. He knew that people tend to see images when under great stress or fear.

Robin had never considered that one of those figures in the cemetery might resemble the expressionless mannequin. She remembered that the face of the mannequin had no features that were apparent behind the mask. Her skin-like material was simply faded and stained white muslin. "Are you saying that someone on your campus and in the community center has a face like the mannequin's? Surely not," she bluntly stated. "How can that be when her face is hidden behind the mask?"

"I had a dream after purchasing it. In my dream, I was painting over the mask. Her features were revealed to me in each stroke of my brush. Yes, the person that I saw had the same physical structure and basic facial features that I had dreamed of.

"Her eyes were very dark and her face was without expression. In addition, her lips had no color to them," he said with a voice that indicated increasing tension within him. "It was as though my dream had taken form."

Robin did not reply to the answer that the Professor provided. It was as if they were talking about two different subjects. Robin thought, "There is no way that any person could resemble the mannequin." Since she had only been looking at the object's back during the discussion, she decided to walk over to the chair upon which it sat. She wanted a closer look. Perhaps she had missed some detail however faint it might be. As she moved closer, she looked into an adjoining mirror dimly lit by the flame of the kerosene lamp. She uttered a small cry. "Have you replaced the mannequin that I saw last night?" she shouted. She did not venture any further having seen its face in the mirror. The mask had been removed to reveal a visage with a piercing stare. She noticed the firelight reflected from the object's eyes – the burning flames within the hearth clearly showing.

Her heart beat strongly as her hands trembled. "Have I grown insane?" she questioned herself. She then blurted out, "The mannequin has facial features now. Are you sure you did not replace it with another?"

The Professor responded, "I am not sure I understand your question. It is the same mannequin I bought on trade day. I can assure you that I did not purchase two of them. Is there something wrong?"

Robin stared at him. "Yesterday and today, when I looked at the mannequin, there were no facial features revealed behind the mask. There were no details or markings of any kind. Today, there is detail and very lifelike facial features."

The Professor said sympathetically, "Robin, you were probably very tired when we arrived at Mt. Ebal last night. Perhaps, you did not look at the mannequin closely enough. I think that the parlor's dim light might have given you the impression that it was featureless. There is always a face behind a mask. Our imagination creates the features. This conversation certainly has gotten interesting. In death, we all become faceless. In myths, considering the role that mirrors have played in contacting the dead, it fits right into the story of Mt. Ebal. I think that we should describe your experience in detail."

Robin replied with a strong voice that shocked him, "This is no longer about a book – it is now a discussion concerning what is reality! I am sure that the mannequin did not have a face yesterday or today until now! You must be using it as a prop to direct the storyline. I suggest that we separate reality from fiction and keep our own dialogues authentic. Without acknowledging the use of props, the process becomes deceitful!"

Noting her strong reaction, the Professor said, "Robin, I can assure you that I am not setting the stage for our discussions. I could have easily written the narrative, utilizing my own props, without inviting you here. There is enough factual information to complete the storyline without resorting to invented plots or subplots."

"Robin, look at it again," said the Professor, still seated. "The mask is in place as it has always been. In the dim light, you only thought you saw a face. The muslin material about her face only hints at her skin tone. In the dim light, you only thought that you saw a face.

"Apparently, she is a mulatto. Of course, it could be that the dyes originally used in the material may have been altered by time and humidity. I am afraid we will never truly know."

Robin spoke softly, "I believe you. I am sorry. I guess I did not study the object closely enough last night or today. The dim light and my fatigue may also have had something to do with it. As you correctly stated, I was very tired when I first saw it."

"What other explanation can there be?" thought Robin. "How can I fail to recall such visually identifying information? There is no way to ever rationalize that there exist two similar mannequins purchased by the Professor." Still, doubt lingered within Robin's mind. She had always prided herself on her excellent recall ability, a gift from her physician father, an ability verified by her extraordinary aptitude for reciting random numbers.

"I don't think we need to rely on mirrors or any other prop to establish the correct emotional setting. You have already provided me with a very vivid idea for our storyline," he said. "We are the storyline."

"I am not following you, Professor."

"I meant to say that we are creating a storyline based in part on happenstance."

- 18 -
THE OUIJA BOARD

The Professor smiled. "Why don't we try the Ouija board? When I last tried it several years ago, it seemed to move on its own. It started to spell the name of an unseen guest but my wife, afraid that it would frighten our son, stopped it. After all, we were trying to convince him that there were no ghosts in the house."

"What do you mean?" asked Robin.

"My son was very much afraid of the house from the first moment he entered it. Like my mother, he sensed that something evil existed within it, something unseen that would grow in its desire to kill. My wife and I thought that we could make him feel better about the house if we staged a Ouija board session in which we were to ask the question, 'Are there any ghosts in the house?'

"When I asked that question, the planchette sped to the word *Yes*. We immediately saw the fear in our son's face. It was a confirmation of his ability to sense a presence unknown to the rest of us. At that point, I put the board away, never to take it out until now."

With hesitation, Robin replied, "I don't know what to think. My answers have been replaced by questions. It frightens me also. In that it is now March 26, the eve of Palm Sunday, I am beginning to think that we are somehow being manipulated, perhaps by our own compulsion to write a novel. As far as the Ouija board is concerned, let's do give it a try. It can't be any more frightening or revealing than the mirrors have been."

The Professor left the room and came back with the board and planchette in hand. He explained, "You might enjoy knowing some of the history behind this Ouija board. It is the very one that we played on the night before the tornado. It is really an antique. I believe that the copyright date is 1898. Both the board and planchette are made from some exotic wood. Well, at least that fellow at the Louisiana trade day told me so.

"My wife and I had spent much of the day looking for Woodlawn Plantation's former site when we came across a most interesting trade day vendor who happened to have a Ouija board for sale." The Professor paused while looking about the parlor. "In that most things in this room were destroyed, I was lucky to find both the board and planchette after the storm. Of course, they were rained on for several days and you can still see the moisture marks on the back of the board."

Robin could see the marks where the varnish had become discolored. She gently rubbed the wood as though attempting to create a charm upon its surface.

Facing each other in straight-backed chairs, both Robin and the Professor placed the board upon their knees, their fingers barely touching the planchette. Their knees brushed against each another's for a brief moment of uneasy familiarization. The fire made snapping sounds as a small fragment of pine tar burned and sparked. The hall clock sounded louder than before. The rain ceased and the tree branches stopped clawing at the roof. There was a profound silence except for the fireplace crackling and the metronomic pacing of the clock. The Professor asked the first question, "Is there an unseen spirit present in the room?"

Both participants closed their eyes and waited.

Slowly at first and then with increasing speed, the planchette moved across the board. Robin and the Professor opened their eyes and watched. Neither one wanted to admit that the instrument was moving forcefully across the board. In silence, both accused the other of orchestrating the event. The planchette stopped while pointed towards *Yes*.

The Professor then asked, "Is the spirit male or female?" Once again the planchette moved quickly to the letter *F*.

The Professor asked Robin to submit the next question.

"If a spirit is present and you are female, please spell your first name," she said. Nothing happened. Both participants looked at the planchette as though it no longer functioned; like a toy whose battery had died. Neither spoke for fear that no further action would occur.

Then slowly the planchette moved away from the letters. It traced the outer limits of the board and returned to point to the letter *A*. They waited for the next letter to be identified. The instrument failed to move. Instantly, a bolt of lightning struck the aged pine in the front yard, traveled down its trunk and tore through the surface of the earth raising a steaming mound of soil. Robin jumped in terror; the board, resting uneasily upon her legs, fell heavily to the floor cracking the wooden planchette into two parts.

The Professor looked at her and said loudly, "It is obvious that we cannot ask any more questions of the Ouija board this evening! I am surprised that the storm has reappeared with such intensity followed now by both wind and lightning. It has repeated this same cycle several times this evening."

A downdraft unexpectedly resulted in a whirlwind of fire in the hearth, forcing burning ash to drift once more into the parlor. The sound of tapping was then heard on the roof as hail began to fall. The Professor clearly remembered that the sound of hail always introduced a destructive storm. Small beads of sweat formed upon his forehead as his mind flashed back to 1994.

The Professor stated, "We all strive to know what is beyond life. It is, perhaps, the greatest mystery of all. Unfortunately, there is no way to prove the existence of the soul one way or the other. We will all know the answer soon enough. Regardless of our desire to believe, there is always the feeling of doubt. The feeling that our partner is attempting to manipulate the Ouija board." the Professor laughed sensing her doubts. "Our desire to believe is equally balanced by our skepticism. We all want to hear the scream in the night; the image in white moving through empty hallways. Only then, can our faith be affirmed.

"At Mt. Ebal, a former renter and her husband lived in the house for more than ten years. They enjoyed each moment of living here, or at least so they said. Since they regarded Mt. Ebal as their permanent home, much to my pleasure since they made excellent renters, they asked my permission to enclose the porch. They assured me that they would build it to duplicate the other portion of the house in order to ensure proper balance as required by the time period in which the original house had been constructed. At the conclusion of their efforts and verified by photographs, the two sides looked identical.

"They painted the interior of the room a lime green color. I had previously asked them to use 1- by 12-inch tongue in groove boards for walls in keeping with the style of many Greek Revival homes constructed in the countryside during that time period. The only oddity in the construction process was that they had chosen to raise the porch floor approximately two inches. I am still not sure why. The quality of the workmanship, however, was exceptional. You could not tell the window frames and other detail work from the original construction. Fortunately for both the renter and myself, he found a contractor that was well versed in restoration carpentry.

"A month after the enclosed room was finished, I received a call from the renter who sounded very anxious. She told me that she and her husband were leaving immediately and just wanted to give me the required 30-day notice. I was shocked considering the great expense that they had voluntarily undergone. When I asked why they were leaving, she said, 'I had a dream. In my dream, a woman was standing above my bed looking down at me. I could not make out the details of her face. I realized that I had been dreaming and upon awakening, I saw her there staring at me in the moonlight, a faceless stare. I screamed loudly for her to leave. Then like in a film, she began to float backwards into the wall of the room."

"I asked her if her husband had also seen the woman. She said no. He had fallen asleep in the parlor while watching a movie.

"I questioned them further about their desire to leave, asking if anything else had occurred to discourage them from remaining. I wanted to know if I could do anything in order to keep them. The renter said that other events had occurred, but she preferred not to discuss them with me. After the call, they moved out in less than two weeks. Oddly enough, they took the antique lock on the hall doors as though intending to return."

The Professor continued, "My farmhouse in Texas has had a very troubled past as I briefly mentioned earlier on our way back from Atlanta. There are several incidences that I have already told you about. One day when visiting the farm to check on the status of the house and pastures, I noticed the renter standing out in the yard staring at the house. I asked him how things were going and he replied that everything was fine except when his girlfriend went to work. He was unemployed and being supported by his common-law wife. I assumed he meant that he missed her very much. I told to him that I too missed my wife when I was younger, but we needed to work to pay for our college expenses. Sometimes we both had to work more than one job and, therefore, spent a great deal of time apart.

"The renter replied, 'As you know, my wife works days in Longview. When she leaves for work, I sit out in the yard and wait for her to get back. I don't care if it is hot or cold, I am in the yard. It is not that I miss her so much; it is that there is something in the house that bothers me. I mean, it scares me. She thinks I am a little crazy, but it is there. I swear it is.'

"I then asked, 'Is your wife also afraid?'

"The renter replied, 'She ain't afraid of nothin'. I would move to Jefferson in a second if I could. It is not that I see something, it is that I sense something that is there.'"

The Professor added, "I didn't want to lose them as renters so I did not ask for further details. It was strange to me at the time that a grown man with a family would be afraid to enter a house during the day based only on what he sensed. We have all been in a house and felt something standing behind us.

"After my conversation with him, two months passed and I didn't receive any rent. At the end of four months, I traveled to Texas to meet with my property manager who had, in the meantime, obtained an eviction notice based on their failure to pay and their failure to notify him concerning their future intentions.

"When we arrived to confront the renters and inspect the house, we found the front door unlocked. After knocking several times, the property manager and I entered the hallway and saw the house still filled with their belongings. The computer had been left on. As we walked through the house, we found clothing strewn about the floor and drawers gaping open. At first we thought that the renters had been robbed. This, however, was not the case for valuable stereo equipment and other electronic components remained in the farmhouse. There were no signs of the occupants. The renters had simply vanished."

The Professor continued, "Sometimes we find evidence to substantiate our beliefs and, equally so, our doubts. You remember me saying that my Texas home had previously burned down. I loved that house just as I do Mt. Ebal. I have had to rent the farmhouse in order to keep it. The property taxes and insurance are too high for me to leave it vacant. Besides, drug users would probably become squatters on the property. The last time it was rented, the house burned. While not completed destroyed, much of it was gutted. The flooring and most of the outside walls were all that remained. At a distance it appeared to be the same house. However, upon entering the house, only charred wood and dripping water greeted us. I learned from Mt. Ebal that as long as you had a floor remaining, you could rebuild the house. I also knew that I could not destroy what remained of the structure.

"A neighbor had spotted the smoke escaping from the farmhouse and called the fire department. The renters, I was to find out later, lost everything in the fire. I too lost several irreplaceable antiques in the house. Once the inferno was extinguished, the fire marshal ordered that nothing be touched until a state-mandated arson investigation was conducted.

"The house sat for several weeks with water still on the floors as I awaited the report. There was no point in my taking annual leave to be there. Finally the investigation was completed with the finding that arson was not a factor in the fire. It was concluded that the fire did in fact start in the room that my mother called the 'cold room.'

"Everyone that looked at the house said that it too, like Mt. Ebal, could not be rebuilt. I choose not to go to Texas to witness the devastation, but instead asked my property manager to see about checking with various contractors to determine if they could provide an estimate or an opinion regarding the house. Only three were willing to travel to the site.

"Being over 600 miles away, I asked each of them to e-mail me pictures of the house to help determine what course of action I should pursue. One contractor did not have a computer and was, therefore, eliminated. The first contractor who inspected the house sent twenty-five images. He informed me that the house could not be saved and the photographs were proof of that fact. As I looked at each image, memories returned. The beautiful wood trim, molding and antique doors were but charred wood. Near the end of my review, one image struck me as very odd. In the official report, the origin of the fire was in the back corner room where a later added turbine had served to fuel the fire with abundant oxygen.

"This was the room that my mother had always described as the 'cold room.' My uncle, who was two years older, and I liked to scare one another in the summer by hiding in the 'cold room' while playing hide-and-seek. It was a room with only one window located on the south side of the house. This room, by its location and lack of air circulation, should have been the hottest room in the house. Instead it was the coolest in summer.

"When the house was built, in all probability, the original site of the room was a wide porch. A cistern that provided the water for the house adjoined the porch at this location. Later, the porch was to be enclosed to form, what my mother referred to as the 'Power Room.'"

"My mother always felt that something evil had happened in the Power Room. She mentioned it to a renter, an artist, who was married to a young woman who had previously studied the occult. My mother had also ventured into the occult as well, but stopped after being warned by my grandmother not to proceed any further into that which was unknown.

"As a professor, Mother had become intrigued by a student's painting. A painting that bothered not only me but my son as well. The painting was very abstract, but if you looked closely at the details, it was possible to imagine seeing people dancing around a fire. Nearby stood a man with a goat's body and horns. For years, it was to hang above my mother's head as she slept. It was later destroyed in the fire.

"The renter's husband told my mother that his wife was a white witch and could only do good. This seemed strange to me in that the husband was a university art professor. You always assume that the occult appeals only to the uneducated. I later noticed that he had drilled holes in the bathroom door so that he could observe a person bathing. Judging from the number of liquor bottles in the ditch across from the house, it was apparent that he had also become an alcoholic, before it was discovered that he had pancreatic cancer.

"Even though the Power Room was on the west side of the house which should have borne the heat of the sun, the artist's wife also noticed that the temperature in the room was much lower than the rest of the house. His wife, upon my mother's suggestion, performed the requested non-church sanctioned exorcism. Afterwards she then declared the room free of evil spirits.

"After her husband's death, I do not know what happened to the artist's wife. She was beautiful and young.

"The photograph that the prospective contractor sent me of the burned farmhouse was most unusual," said the Professor as he showed the image on his laptop to Robin. "The mere fact that the fire started in this particular room was disturbing enough. As you can see, two people appear in the photograph. The smaller image is of a woman in what appears to be a picture frame. The other image is of more concern. At first, I thought that someone was just standing inside the window in the burned room. I could not, however, imagine what the images were doing in the photograph. They had nothing to do with my rebuilding the house. I enlarged the images only to find them even more disturbing. Enlarged, they were very frightening. I felt that I was looking at a demon and the person killed in the room. Perhaps her body had been placed in the porch cistern located directly beneath her portrait. Later I was to see that the well curb had been burned away revealing the dark water and crumbling brickwork.

"I know that the photograph does not prove anything, yet I cannot explain it. The contractor never made a reference to it either in his e-mails or phone calls. True, the quality of the images he sent were not excellent, but it demonstrated to me that he lacked the sophistication to have altered any of the images, much less created special effects. And for what purpose would such a staging have served?

"Since the contractor felt that the house could not be saved, I ended up with another builder that completed the task. Several items, including the antique doors stored in the barn, were later stolen from the building site but nothing occult was ever reported."

Robin, like the Professor, enlarged the image on the computer to its maximum. She too assumed that it had been staged but, on closer inspection, the two figures within the image became more disconcerting. She could sense the horror that the supposed victim must have felt.

"When magnified, there appears to be a growth on the woman's neck. What can it be?" asked Robin.

"It was common in that area of Texas when salt was not yet iodized. To me, this would not have been unusual in that earlier time period. As a child, I often saw women with such growths in the nearby farming community," said the Professor.

Robin leaned back in her chair and stared at the screen. The Professor closed the laptop without further comments regarding the image.

The Professor continued, "The next strange incident involved a male renter that managed a daycare center in a nearby community. I never met nor did I ever see the man who lived alone, but there was something different about how the house looked whenever I visited the site. The doors were always open without any screens to keep out the insects. When I shouted to see if anyone was there, I was greeted only by the sound of a television set being cut on the moment I shouted. The yard always contained children's toys that were broken and discarded. In the front yard was the large sign *Paw Paw's No Spanking Zone.*

"Like the last tenants at Mt. Ebal, three renters had left abruptly and at a financial loss to both themselves and me. I could never figure out their need to leave so abruptly. What had terrified them so? I assumed that it was only their imagination."

Robin and the Professor, ignoring once more the storm outside, remained at the table drinking the locally grown sweet wine. Their discussion turned to travel and Robin's family concerns. Her son was completing a tour in Afghanistan. His marine battalion came under fire just as he was scheduled to depart. Because of casualties in the unit and the need for debriefings, his orders were extended for four additional weeks. Instead of coming to Mt. Ebal, she was hoping to spend R&R time with him in Hawaii. What was to have been a period of readjustment did not take place. Disappointed, Robin hoped that her journey to Mt. Ebal would provide repose from her concerns.

The Professor had not, up to this point, discussed his own family. Robin earlier noticed the painting above the fireplace. "Is the painting that of your wife and child?"

The Professor's only response was, "Yes." It was apparent that he did not wish to discuss this particular subject in any detail. An uncomfortable silence followed.

Robin replied, "You have, I mean, had a very nice-looking family." She felt very awkward having made such a thoughtless comment. She only hoped that he understood her intentions.

The Professor looked away towards the large mirror that reflected the mannequin's image. "Thank you," he responded.

Robin herself looked towards the fireplace where the flame was now dying from neglect. "I am very tired. Would you mind if I prepare for bed?"

The Professor did not look at her. "Certainly, I laid out some fresh linen. I will light another lamp for you. I hope that you have a very good night's rest." With that comment, Robin excused herself from the table.

- 19 -
DREAMS

As Robin walked towards her room, her silhouette preceding her, she could hear the hail hitting the metal roof. A loud popping sound came from the fireplace and then the house was quiet except for the renewed sound of static. "The Professor must have cut the old black-and-white television set on again. That's strange," she thought. "We are in the house, so why would he be concerned about intruders? It must be out of habit. Somewhat like a white noise machine that people use to drown out unwanted sounds."

Robin entered the bathroom and prepared to bathe. She was still uncomfortable with the lack of privacy shades or blinds on the windows. The large mirrors also irritated her by making her appear distorted, which she assumed was due to the manufacturing processes used many years ago.

The hot water felt very good and relaxed her even more. Soon she was asleep in the warm waters of the tub. She was immediately back in the cemetery. This time she was very close to the three people working around the graves. She could see the faces of the men. Young and very good looking in their uniforms. Tall with black hair and full beards very much like the illustrations of Civil War soldiers that she had seen in an old Currier and Ives publication belonging to her great grandmother. The woman in the cemetery was much smaller. Her face remained concealed as she tended the graves alongside her companions. In her hand was a very old, rust-covered sickle. Her dress, a black coarse material befitting the time period, was full length. While unable to see her face, Robin thought there was something very familiar about her as if she were a person that she must have known. Robin could not make out the names on the graves that they were clearing the saplings and wildflowers from. Instead of wisteria and honeysuckle, there was the strong odor of lavender.

The three images were silent as they work, their hoes and sickles rising in rhythmic sync. Robin noticed the sky becoming increasingly dark as black clouds boiled over the landscape. Slowly the woman turned her head towards Robin, pupils aflame, her face pallid and emotionless.

Robin suddenly awakened from her dream. Her nose had gone under the water, filling her throat and bronchial area with soapy water. Coughing, she noticed that the bathwater had grown cold. She wondered how long she had been asleep. The sweet smell of lavender remained suspended in the moist air of the bathroom. Rain did not cease beating against the windowpanes.

Upon emerging from her bath, she saw herself in the full mirror. Her figure was unrecognizable in the lamplight and the distortions of the antique reflective surface. No matter how she positioned herself, her face remained ill-defined. She adorned her house shoes, gown and reentered the bedroom.

As she lay there, she thought she could hear the Professor speaking to someone. Robin could not make out the words, but he seemed to be engaged in a conversation. She thought this very strange in that she had not heard a knock on the door or the opening and closing of the entryway doors. Perhaps, the rabbit ears on the old television had picked up a strong enough signal to allow the audio to be heard. With this comforting rationalization, she was soon asleep and with it, another dream rapidly occurred.

ര

Suddenly the painting that the Professor had verbally described became real. Musical instruments sounded as the painted images danced around the fire. Tambourines, mitbiq, and buzuq played loudly. The fire around which they danced and played their musical instruments crackled and shot forth abundant sparks. Soon the dancing troop bowed as an unknown creature appeared in the mist of the dance – man, goat and demon all in one. Immediately, Robin found herself dancing naked before the horned image, her hair swirling to the sounds that accompanied the dance. She became an image within the painting.

ଔ

She awoke startled and then stared at the bedroom ceiling. She reached for the glass of water by her bed, sipped it slowly and then once more could not resist falling asleep. The double doors of the bedroom swung open; the light was brilliant on the porch. She looked around and immediately saw herself seated before a white table whose surface had images and incomplete sentences carved upon it. A cup of tea had been poured; a bowl of flowers prepared – roses, honeysuckle and marigolds. The air was filled with the scent of lavender. A gold necklace with a very small cameo surrounded by pearls hung from her neck. The colonel she had seen in the cemetery stood on the porch before her in full dress uniform. A silver and gold sword dangled from his wide leather belt. His eyes were filled with excitement; his expression one of happiness. He laughed with kindness as he gazed down at her. "This morning I picked wildflowers for you. This evening I will line our bed with roses," he said. "Today is our wedding day. Annie, I have waited a lifetime for this day. I know I should not see you before the wedding, but I never want to leave your presence."

Startled, Robin awoke. The room felt unfamiliar to her and very cold.

ଔ

In the nearby parlor sat the Professor. The television had come on by itself following a nearby lightning strike. This in and of itself was not unusual except for the very clear audio portion that consisted of a man and a woman talking about their future and their love for one another. It was obviously a very old film based on the tone of their conversation. After having cut the set off, the Professor seated himself before the fireplace. He stroked the hot red ashes to garner as much heat as possible from the dying fire. The ashes swirled in the hearth as a downdraft once more forced smoke into the room.

Seated to his left side was the mannequin. He thought about how ridiculous it was not to have stored it in the caboose. What purpose did it now serve? Its presence had obviously disturbed Robin. He did not want to admit it, but he was growing increasingly attracted to her. He now felt the need to protect her.

With the realization that he had begun to care for Robin, he decided to remove the mannequin from the parlor. He thought, "I will put it in the hallway, so I can remember to move it to the caboose in the morning. I will explain to Robin that since she is here, there is no need to convince others that the house is occupied. I will put it back in its former position once she leaves."

He rose from his chair and looked directly into the cracked mirror from Galveston that rested upon the mantel. Within the mirror, he could clearly see himself. Yet dimly seen behind his image, three other people appeared to be standing. He immediately turned around only to see the empty room and the mannequin. "It must be my imagination," he reasoned. Even though he was convinced that he had just experienced a brief mental illusion originating from his having gotten up too quickly combined with his too eager consumption of alcohol, his pulse now pounded loudly within his ears.

He did not look at the mirror again but as he attempted to pick up the mannequin, the book she had been clutching for so many years fell to the floor. He lowered the mannequin back onto the chair and reached over to pick up the leather-bound book. The leather felt soft – an indication of its age and deterioration. Pieces of the leather binding fell to the floor.

He touched his shirt pocket, trying to find his glasses but they were not there. He walked to his desk, but they were not there either. He flipped the aged book over to read the title of the book. Without his glasses, he was forced to squint. The title read *My Visit to Mt. Ebal House, 1863*. On the first page, he read *Annie's Diary*. His hands shaking, he flipped through the remaining pages looking for entries.

Each page, he soon discovered, was blank until the last page of the book. There, handwritten in beautiful print, were only three lines:

Colonel Jeffery Phillip Renfro, 1838 – 1863
Miss Annie Fuller Finch, 1840 – 1863
Lieutenant Gregory Fuller Haynes, 1840 – 1863

At first the Professor could not understand what he had just read. How could a book obtained at a remote trade day possibly have a reference to Mt. Ebal? He also found it very odd that Annie's last name was the same as Robin's. "Could Robin somehow have removed the book, made the entries and placed it back in the mannequin's hands?" he asked himself. "Perhaps she decided to stage events herself. That has to be it since she accused me of doing the same."

The clock struck. The slow count of the hour was unusually loud as both the sound of the fireplace and the earlier conversation had ended. It was now midnight on Palm Sunday.

"How could she have removed the book?" he wondered. "I tried on several occasions to release the mannequin's grip, and the vendor claimed he also tried to detach it without success. Perhaps we loosened it enough for Robin to remove and make the entries. No, that too doesn't make sense, but it is the only plausible explanation."

He looked in the direction of the porch, for a strong light could be seen entering the hallway. Uneasy, the Professor walked towards the light. He emerged onto the porch in morning sunlight. There before him seated at the table was Robin in a white full-length dress. A gold necklace with a very small circular object of brilliant gold surrounded by pearls hung from her neck. Her hair was tightly worn in a bun. Before her was a teapot and, on the table, an arrangement of wildflowers. The Professor seated himself. Carved upon the wood of the tabletop were poems that he recognized as having written himself. The sweet smell of lavender floated in the air.

ଓଃ

Immediately, the scene changed. A strong cold wind moved an embroidered cloth that now covered the table, hiding the poetry that had been written upon its surface. He felt a fine mist of cool rain on his cheeks.

Robin said, "Colonel, how are you feeling today? You didn't come to my bed last night. I assume that you must have fallen asleep by the fireplace while reading."

"Annie," the Colonel replied, "I am sorry, the fire felt so good, and I was very tired. I was with General Forrest yesterday at Centre. We won the fight but several friends were killed. I didn't want to mention it to you since I knew it would only bother you. I kept thinking about Robert and Joe Rich until I fell asleep. They were brothers. Their plantation is not too far from here. I had their bodies taken to their mother yesterday evening. I will need to attend their funeral tomorrow afternoon. I am sorry, but they will need to be buried quickly."

The Colonel continued, "I didn't want you to know about the battle and the losses until after our marriage. This day is to be the happiest of days for you. I love you very much."

Suddenly, Colonel Renfro and Annie could hear a rider rapidly ascending to Mt. Ebal from the road below. The sound of a galloping horse immediately brought back the memory of battlefield scenes.

Upon the rise, before the house, appeared Lt. Gregory Haynes, his black beard hiding his youthful face. Dust drifted before the rider as his horse rose to greet the swirling clouds.

The stallion reared once more as he shouted, "Colonel! Tornado!"

ଓ

The tornado arrived at 11:00 the morning of March 27. There was little warning of what was to take place. The Professor realized that he had ignored all the signs of the approaching storm: the wind, lightning, hail and the whirlwinds within the fireplace.

In the cemetery, new graves arrived as the victims of the storm were buried. With many children dead, several of the markers contained but scant information. Several loved ones placed a small lamb between the birth and death dates of the children.

After the storm, no one claimed Robin's body. The local church provided the funds for her funeral. Just a few faculty members attended the Professor's funeral from the local university. They were buried next to each other in a common plot that had been previously purchased by the church for itinerant workers. A third victim, a church member who had gone to warn them, was buried next to them. Soon weeds, wildflowers and saplings covered their unattended graves.

Epilogue

After the tornado that destroyed both Mt. Ebal and the adjoining church, I visited the site of the house again. Today, Mt. Ebal sits as a ruin. The thick pine forest grows ever closer to the steps. Crows move about the abandoned driveway. The Professor's car rusts in silence, its windows shattered by the flying rocks and later by vandals. Shreds from the seat covers flop in the wind. Slowly the remaining windowpanes of the house cracked under the stress of decay.

The walls began to sag under the unrelenting passage of seasons with their cycles of heat and cold. Rain from winter storms and spring downpours added to the soft symphony of decay. Paint peeled off, revealing the heart pine that had postponed its own destruction for two hundred years. Lizards ran across the lattes where the plaster had let go. The vivid colors of the walls were now turned into pastels. Wasps, carpenter bees and centipedes could not resist the deteriorating wood. Mice could be heard scurrying upon my approach.

I could not help but turn over some of the boards strewn about the yard. I did not know what I was looking for beneath the mixture of decay that greeted me. Spiders dwelt beneath the rotten boards. Perhaps I was looking for some communication from my friend – a photograph or a written article. Something that would provide an answer to the myriad questions that formed since I found the aged book in the library.

After having removed several heavy planks, I found a leather-bound book similar to the one that I had first located in the library. The leather stuck to my fingers as I attempted to open the pages now stiffened by rain and time. As I broke the pages apart, I recognized the handwriting of the Professor. I also noted that the last two pages were written in a different ink as well as handwriting style. It was as though two people had written in the journal. "How could that be?" I thought.

My curiosity extended to the young woman whose body was also found in the debris after the tornado. Her identification indicated that she was from the northeast. I cannot understand why she was in the house at the time the tornado struck.

Initially, the fire department and police thought they had found a fourth victim when they noticed a hand protruding from underneath the collapsed chimney. Upon further investigation, they determined that it was the hand of a mannequin protruding above the bricks cast by the collapsing chimney. I was told later that the mannequin was sold to a vendor who attended trade days. I think that my friend said Lost Graves trade day or some such name as that.

Before I could begin reading the contents of the book, a car angled its way up the abandoned driveway to Mt. Ebal. A young faculty member and his wife emerged from the automobile. He greeted me with a smile. "We didn't expect to find you here, Professor. We were just driving by, enjoying the fall weather, when we noticed a FOR SALE sign posted on the property gate. Are you interested in buying this property or just looking?" inquired the young faculty member respectfully, careful not to intrude upon a colleague's personal intent.

"No, Clyde, just looking at the site. As you know, we fellow historians cannot pass by an old structure without examining it," I replied.

"Professor, how did you know that the road led to an abandoned house?" asked Clyde.

"I knew the person that used to live here several years ago. I remember having been invited to a party at Mt. Ebal. The house was very interesting from a historical perspective. In fact, the owner taught in the History Department."

"What a perfect day to be outside," responded Clyde. "Heather, I love this spot. You can see for miles above the treetops. As you can see, some walls and a fireplace remain from the previous structure.

Based on the pegs used to join the sills, it must be really old. I wonder if we could add onto the remaining portion of the house. I also noticed an old mantelpiece still above the fireplace. It is weather-stained and the mirror is cracked, but I might be able to dress it up. You know, we could have the best of both worlds living here – the old and the new." He spoke hesitantly awaiting her rebuttal.

Her response surprised him. "Now that you are an assistant professor, do what you want to. I know you will, anyway," she said with a coquettish smile. "It is going to take a lot of work just to clean the site and level the foundation. Do you think we could have the house finished by the following spring? It would be great to have it ready to move into before the mountain dogwoods bloom. Around spring break would be fantastic. Springtime here must be really beautiful."

"Heather," asked the Professor, "where is your home?"

"I am from Lakeville, Connecticut. Once you have lived in the country among the trees, it is difficult to live anywhere else. My parents had a very old colonial home there. I remember it very well. You know, old homes have their own personalities, just like people."

A noise came from within the pile of bricks that had been the chimney. "I am sure that wild animals must love this place," said Clyde.

I could only reply, "Yes."

The History Of A Storm

At 11:22 a.m. on March 27, 1994 occurred the most deadly tornado outbreak in modern Alabama history. The funnel dropped from a small isolated cell over the lake at Ohatchee, Alabama. The killing force did not end until it had cut across much of northeast Alabama and north Georgia. Mt. Ebal house was in the path of the F4 tornado, later referred to in the press as the Palm Sunday Tornado. The tragedy gained national attention leading then Vice President Al Gore to view the destruction from a low-flying helicopter.

This tornado was especially tragic for it destroyed, among others, eleven churches and killed twenty-two children who were preparing for an Easter pageant at the Goshen Methodist Church. One of the children killed was the daughter of the minister. It was as though a hand had drawn a line connecting the churches, targeting their members. The Palm Sunday tornado was only one of several events that were to impact the residents of the house that had been moved from Dahlonega Street in Ladigaville, Alabama to the top of Mt. Ebal, a small mountain in the Appalachian foothills. I look back at all of the incidences that, now seen from the present, indicated that a tragic event was about to occur. A storm accurately referred to as "evil."

APPENDIX

All that remains of the magnificent 30-room Galveston Mansion –
a small fragment of the mirror frame.

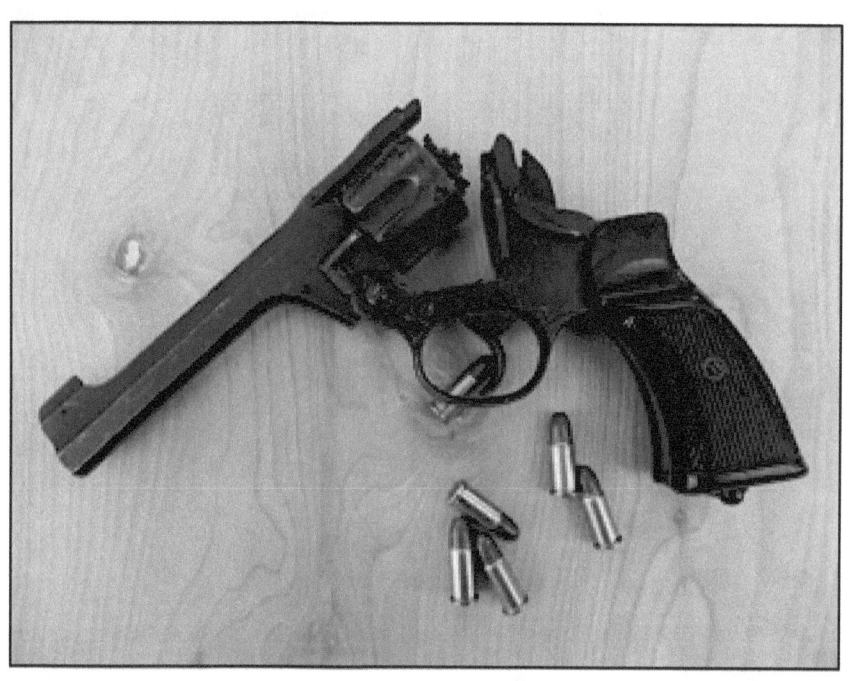

The Professor's revolver,
used to confront the unholy one, recovered from the debris field.

Terror within the cold room. Images from the burned farmhouse.
Photograph taken by unknown contractor.

About The Author

Franklin Lafayette King, Jr. was born in the Panhandle of Texas and spent much of his youth on the Blackland Prairie. He received a commission through the University of Texas in Austin and soon became involved in the Vietnam Conflict. After additional academic preparation, he moved to the foothills of the Appalachians. In addition to combat, he experienced both the eyes of a hurricane and an F-4 tornado, events that were to influence much of his later work. Mr. King is a frequent visitor to Europe from which much of the inspiration for this book was derived. He is the author of *In the Shadow of Leaves, The Seven Woods of Coole, The Woman in the Window, Sunflowers and Zinnias, Hauntings of a Summer Moon* and *The Poet Who Writes upon Water* – all published by Texture Press.

www.ingramcontent.com/pod-product-compliance
Lightning Source LLC
Chambersburg PA
CBHW020653260626
47157CB00008B/3014